The Cold Light Of Day...

Halley awoke sometime before dawn. She was curled up with her back against Jay's chest, warm and secure, and she sighed with contentment. It was only as she came more fully awake that she realized something was wrong with this picture, and she remembered exactly what had happened last night....

Surprisingly she felt no guilt, no regret. How could she, when last night was nothing short of delicious as they'd remembered their shared passions? What was more, through their physical closeness they had opened the door for further communication—something they'd had precious little of before the divorce.

The divorce. Now that was something they couldn't ignore. When they had decided to officially end their marriage, it had seemed there had been no alternative. Had anything really changed since then?

Well, the divorce was a done deed. They couldn't go back and undo it....

Or could they?

Dear Reader:

Sensuous, emotional, compelling . . . these are all words that describe Silhouette Desire. If this is your first Desire novel, let me extend an invitation for you to sit back, kick off your shoes and revel in the pleasure of a tantalizing, fulfilling love story. If you're a regular reader, you already know that you're in for a real treat!

A Silhouette Desire can encompass many varying moods and tones. The story can be deeply moving and dramatic, or charming and lighthearted. But no matter what, each and every Silhouette Desire is a terrific romance written by and for today's woman.

I know you'll love March's *Man of the Month* book, *McAllister's Lady* by Naomi Horton. Also, look for *Granite Man*, one of Elizabeth Lowell's WESTERN LOVERS series. And don't miss wonderful love stories by some undeniable favorites *and* exciting newcomers: Kelly Jamison, Lucy Gordon, Beverly Barton and Karen Leabo.

So give in to Desire . . . you'll be glad you did!

All the best,

Lucia Macro
Senior Editor

KAREN LEABO

CLOSE QUARTERS

SILHOUETTE *Desire®*

Published by Silhouette Books New York

America's Publisher of Contemporary Romance

SILHOUETTE BOOKS
300 East 42nd St., New York, N.Y. 10017

CLOSE QUARTERS

ISBN: 0-373-05629-X

First Silhouette Books printing March 1991

Books by Karen Leabo

Silhouette Romance

Roses Have Thorns #648
Ten Days in Paradise #692
Domestic Bliss #707
Full Bloom #731
Smart Stuff #764

Silhouette Desire

Close Quarters #629

KAREN LEABO

credits her fourth-grade teacher with initially spark-
ing her interest in creative writing. She was determined at an early age to have her work published.
When Karen was in the eighth grade she wrote a chil-
dren's book and convinced her school yearbook publisher to put it in print.

Karen was born and raised in Dallas but now lives
in Kansas City, Missouri. She has worked as a magazine art director, a free-lance writer and a textbook
editor, but now she keeps herself busy full-time writing about romance.

This book is dedicated to my critique groups
(including Judy Manelis and her lesson on verbs).

Prologue

Snow fell in thick lace curtains by the time Halley Jernigan's transatlantic flight made a cautious landing at New York's JFK airport. As the wheels touched down on the icy runway without mishap, Halley breathed a grateful sigh. Now that she'd landed safely, she could declare her six-week foray into the European fashion world an unqualified success. The Mystique Modeling Agency, already a formidable entity in New York, was making a name for itself on an international level.

Still, Halley was glad the trip was over. She'd had quite enough of her four traveling companions. Squiring a bevy of teenage fashion models all over Europe was no small chore. They were attractive, vivacious, and a lot more cheeky than Halley had been at seventeen or eighteen. Just keeping them in their own beds at night had been a challenge.

As the 747 taxied toward the gate, Halley pulled a small mirror from her suede purse and frowned into it. She felt rumpled and gritty. With practiced efficiency she made some quick repairs to her makeup, then coiled her dark mahogany hair into an expert twist. The finishing touch was a green cashmere beret, secured atop her hair at a saucy angle. She took one final peek in the mirror and deemed her appearance acceptable.

"How do you *do* that, Halley?" one of the girls asked in awe. "You've been on a plane for eight hours and you look like you're ready for a photo session."

"Years of practice," Halley answered, gazing with disapproval at her travel-worn charge. "You never know when a camera might appear," she added as a light rebuke. Image was everything in this business, and she couldn't pound that fact into her models' heads often enough.

Chagrined, the young model took a swipe with a brush at her own mussed hair.

The other three girls were already standing in the aisle, chattering about school and boyfriends as they waited impatiently for the hatch to open. Their ceaseless energy, normally a source of amusement for Halley, wore on her frayed nerves this morning.

Customs went smoothly enough, considering the amount of luggage involved. As soon as everyone had cleared that hurdle, Halley ushered her party into the terminal. Almost immediately each of the girls squealed with delight as they fell into the waiting arms of the friends or family who'd come to meet them.

No one waited to hug Halley.

Her throat constricted as a wave of loneliness washed over her. She hadn't known how difficult it would be to arrive home without Jay to welcome her. But she would have to get used to it; as of yesterday Jay was no longer her husband.

She clutched at her shredding composure long enough to give each of her models one last affectionate hug before they hurried off to resume their lives. It was only when she was settled in the back seat of a taxi, with densely falling snow to shield her from public view, that she allowed herself a few quiet tears.

It's just stress, she told herself. Stress and a pinch of self-pity.

"You okay, lady?" the driver asked as he pulled into traffic, tires spinning on the slick concrete.

"Fine," she managed, dabbing at her eyes with a linen handkerchief. She gave him the Mystique Agency's Manhattan address in a tone of voice that indicated she did not want any sympathy.

All she wanted was to soak in a hot bath and sleep for a week. Unfortunately at the moment she wasn't sure she had a bath or a bed she could call her own. But if Harold Dempsey had carried out her instructions with his usual efficiency, the key to her new apartment would be waiting for her at the office. Harold, her administrative assistant and bookkeeper, had graciously agreed to take care of moving her things while she was in Europe.

Halley paid the cab driver, enticing him with a generous tip to carry her bags all the way into the Korman Building lobby. It felt good to be back, she thought as she stepped into the brass- and oak-trimmed elevator. The luxurious trappings of the building that housed her agency were a comforting reminder that her business was prospering. During the past few difficult months she had clung to her professional success like an anchor as the failures in her personal life had reached a painful crisis point.

The elevator doors opened onto the eighteenth floor. Dragging her suitcases behind her, Halley walked the ten steps to the agency's front entrance and grabbed on to the brass doorknob, bracing herself for the usual round of disasters that always came to light when she returned from a business trip.

Kathryn was waiting for her in the foyer, sitting stiffly at her station behind the polished birch reception desk. She looked up with a sharp intake of breath when the door opened. The stricken expression on her freckled face was all Halley needed to know that she wasn't facing any garden-variety disasters. Something dreadful was wrong.

"Halley, thank goodness you're back. Did you get the message I left for you at the airport?"

Numbly Halley shook her head. Her fingers, still cold from the outdoors, trembled as she undid the fastenings of her blue fox coat. She shrugged out of the fur, her eyes never leaving Kathryn's. When the receptionist remained miserably silent, Halley prodded her. "Did someone die?"

Kathryn took a deep breath. "Worse."

Halley flung her coat over the arm of a chair in an impatient gesture. Kathryn had an irritating habit of drawing out bad news. "C'mon, don't leave me in suspense. What happened?"

"Okay, um, we got a call from the bank yesterday afternoon saying our operating funds account was overdrawn."

Halley put a hand to her forehead and shut her eyes tightly, holding on to her temper by a mere thread. "Uh-huh. And?"

"Well I knew it had to be some kind of mistake, so I tried to find Harold so he could straighten it out, and—well, I couldn't find him. Anywhere. He's gone . . . and so is all the money."

"Gone? Gone where?" As understanding dawned, shock, anger, and disbelief vied for control of Halley's reaction. Anger won out. "What exactly are you saying?" she demanded sharply. "You can't possibly imagine that Harold Dempsey . . ."

"Is an embezzler," Kathryn finished. "I'm not imagining it, either. He took everything. The rent's overdue, so's the insurance, and even the payroll checks are b-bouncing..." Abruptly she started to cry in great, heaving, silent sobs.

Halley grasped Kathryn's hand and squeezed, as much to keep her own tears at bay as to comfort the younger woman. Kathryn Simmons had been with her from the very beginning four years ago. They had coped with lots of crises over the years, but nothing like this. "Have you called the police?" Halley asked at last, struggling for a steady voice.

"Yes, I did that right away," Kathryn replied, brushing her tears away with the back of her hand, smearing her mascara in the process. "They weren't too helpful. They're trying to trace Harold, but they think he's already left the country. South America, probably."

"Oh, God." As the reality of the situation sank in, Halley walked on wooden legs to a soft leather chair and dropped into it, suddenly bone weary. "Oh, God," she said again, trembling uncontrollably.

One

"**H**ow long are you going to fiddle with those lights?"

Jay Jernigan looked up from where he sat on the floor, adjusting a voltage regulator. His partner, Peg Zimmerman, stood over him like a great horned owl ready to pounce on her prey. Her frizzy brown hair stuck out at all angles, causing her to appear slightly deranged, and she had opted to wear her thick glasses today instead of her contacts. The glasses made her eyes look enormous.

"Well?" she demanded.

"Till I get them right. Is there a problem?"

"It's almost seven o'clock."

"So?"

"So, when are you going home?"

"Later," Jay replied vaguely, returning his attention to the voltage regulator.

"You aren't fooling me, you big, dumb Swede," Peg said suddenly, squatting down so she could bring him to eye level. Her brown quilted cape billowed briefly around her, adding to her owlish impression. "You've been sleeping in the darkroom."

"So what if I have?" he replied with feigned disinterest, refusing to rise to her insults. She was the only person in the world who could get away with insulting him to his face, and only because she did it with the best of intentions.

"You're afraid to go home, aren't you?"

"I am not *afraid* of anything. I just have a lot of work to do."

"What work? Seebolt Hardware? We've been doing that catalog for eight years now. You can shoot it in your sleep."

Jay pushed himself off the floor and turned his back on Peg. He sauntered to where his camera and tripod were set up, carefully stepping over the snaking electrical wires, then hit the shutter release. A blinding flash followed. With an emphatic jerk he extracted a Polaroid print from the camera.

"Are you going to talk to me or not?" Peg demanded, quickly covering the physical distance Jay had put between them.

"Not."

"Fine. Keep everything bottled up inside. Get ulcers. See if I care." She stalked away.

"Peg, wait!" Jay called after her.

She stopped before she could reach the door, but she didn't turn around.

"You do care. I know that. But there's nothing to talk about, really. I just have to get used to Halley not being at home."

Peg crossed her arms, tapping her foot on the wooden warehouse flooring.

"I'll go home tonight, I promise. No more sleeping in the darkroom."

The foot-tapping slowed, then stopped. "All right. But you'd better straighten up, Swede. I don't care to work ten hours a day with a man who doesn't open his mouth except to snarl." With that parting comment, the closest she had ever come to a threat, she left.

Jay knew Peg was right. He'd been avoiding the town-house for weeks on end. It wasn't so much that he wanted to avoid Halley—she was seldom there anyway. As soon as they'd filed for divorce she'd packed up all her belongings. Then she'd made herself scarce via several lengthy business trips until the apartment she wanted became available.

Maybe it was the sense of emptiness he was trying to avoid. He couldn't stand the sight of all those boxes.

It was time he returned home on a permanent basis, now that Halley and all her things were gone for good. At least, he assumed they were gone. The movers had been sched-uled to come a couple of days ago.

He peeled the backing off the black-and-white print and set it aside without even looking at it. The decision made, Jay was suddenly in a hurry to go home and face his de-mons.

One by one he turned out all the lights. He shrugged into his down jacket and set the burglar alarm. When he was sure all was secure, he stepped outside and closed the studio door behind him. He was surprised to see almost two feet of snow on the ground. When had that happened? he wondered, looking down at his inadequate tennis shoes. Of course there wasn't a taxi within miles.

By the time he arrived at the narrow, tree-lined street in Greenwich Village where he lived, his shoes were full of melting snow. Despite the discomfort, he didn't rush to the warmth inside but paused to stare up at the tidy pink brick row house that was the home he had shared with Halley for the past six years. They had been deliriously happy there, once upon a time. Shaking his head, he walked the last few steps and with clumsy gloved hands unlocked the dead bolts, stomping to keep the circulation going as he cursed the cold.

When he got the door open, he charged inside—and tripped on an unidentified obstacle sitting right in his path.

He hit the tiled floor with a bang, landing painfully on his elbow. "What the hell?" He sat up, rubbing his throbbing arm as his eyes focused on the offending obstacle, which turned out to be a suitcase.

Halley's suitcase.

"Oh jeez, don't tell me..." But as Jay peered into the living room, he could see that the piles of boxes hadn't been moved an inch. "Halley, are you here?" he called out. Silence answered him.

He didn't need this, he thought as he pulled off his sopping shoes and socks, then maneuvered to his feet. If it weren't so cold outside, he would have turned around and headed right back to the studio.

Why couldn't she just clear out and get it over with, instead of dragging this move out interminably? It wasn't because she wasn't anxious to be gone. Once she had put down a deposit on the swanky Upper East Side apartment, she'd seemed excited about it. It was certainly much better suited to her fast-track life-style than their modest, homey nest in the Village.

As he removed his jacket and scarf, Jay again surveyed the mountain of cardboard cartons in the living room. Maybe that fussy administrative assistant of Halley's wasn't as efficient as she claimed. He couldn't be, or he would have seen that her things were moved, as he'd promised.

The presence of the suitcases bothered him. He couldn't remember seeing them before, but he wasn't certain about anything at this point. "Halley?" he called out again, just to be sure she wasn't here. Again he got no response.

He returned his attention to his cold feet. Now that the numbness was wearing off, his toes tingled painfully. He needed some dry socks.

He didn't bother to turn on the light when he entered the bedroom. He opened the top drawer of his dresser and grabbed a pair of thick wool socks, then sat on the edge of the bed to put them on.

Much better, he thought, wiggling his toes. As he started to push himself off the bed, his hand came in contact with something hard and unyielding. A foot. He sprang up with a surprised yelp and lunged for the light switch, but as soon as he saw the fall of dark hair spilling out across the pillow, he recovered his wits.

Halley. So she *was* here.

He was calm now, but his heart continued to thunder inside his chest. Even asleep, she did things to his nervous system, especially when he hadn't expected to see her.

He stood frozen in one spot for a few moments, just staring at her. She had one leg drawn up with the knee against her chest and the other stretched out, her habitual sleeping position. One slender arm was curved around a pillow, hugging it close. And Jay realized with a start that she was still in her street clothes.

Something was wrong. If there was one thing he knew about Halley, it was that she never simply fell into bed carelessly. She had a strict nighttime regimen that involved removing makeup, applying moisturizer, and brushing out her hair. Jay had taken great delight in watching her do all those things. He could have sat for hours just gazing on her as she ran the bristles of her silver-backed brush through the thick, shiny strands of hair—hair that was such a dark shade of auburn that it was almost black.

Sometimes she had deliberately teased him, sitting at her dressing table in nothing but a teddy, stroking the dark tresses until he was nearly crazy with wanting her. And then

she'd lain the brush down and moved to the bed with pur-
poseful strides, every bit as excited as he was. . . .

He shook his head to dispel the image. Halley obviously
hadn't indulged in any rituals this evening. Her hair was
tangled, with hairpins still clinging here and there. When Jay
looked closer, he could see she hadn't removed her makeup, nor even her jewelry. She had managed to take off her
coat, which was crumpled on the floor next to the bed, but
he'd bet she was fully dressed under the blankets. He didn't
trust himself to check, however, just in case she wasn't.

Could she be ill? He felt her forehead, relieved to find that
it was cool and dry. He let his hand linger against her
smooth skin for a second longer than necessary, trying to
decide if he should awaken her.

In the end, he pulled his hand away without disturbing
her. The mauve shadows under her eyes were testimony to
her exhaustion. He'd let her sleep. But when she woke, he'd
see to it that her things were moved immediately, even if he
had to carry boxes himself.

Halley dreamed she was sitting at her favorite booth at
Ling's, and the waiter had just placed a steaming dish of
pepper beef in front of her. She heaped spoonfuls of the
Oriental delicacy onto moist white rice, then proceeded to
stuff a huge bite into her mouth. But when her lips closed
around the chopsticks, she tasted nothing. Frustrated, she
got another bite, but again when she put it into her mouth,
it disappeared.

Gradually she came awake in the darkened room, realizing with a pang of disappointment that the food was just a
fantasy—but the tantalizing aroma was very real. There was
pepper beef somewhere in this house and she was going to
find it.

She sat up decisively, coming fully awake. The smell of Chinese food could mean only one thing. Jay was home. Did he even know she was here?

Her stomach growled insistently as she slid out from under the covers. She tiptoed out the bedroom door and into the hallway, pausing at the entrance to the living room. Jay sat on the floor with his back to her, leaning over the marble-topped coffee table and devouring what had to be food from Ling's. His oversized cable-knit sweater hung invitingly over his broad shoulders and muscular back. His thick blond hair reached past his collar, longer than Halley could remember seeing it. He forgot to get it cut when she wasn't around to remind him, she decided with a flash of womanly possessiveness.

"Jay?"

Though she spoke his name softly, his shoulders hunched up in surprise and his fork clattered to the table. "Halley, what are you doing here?" he said without turning around. "I thought by now you'd be firmly ensconced in your pricey penthouse."

"It's not a penthouse," she replied, biting her lip to control the urge to hurl an angry retort.

The warmth of the fire in the wood-burning stove drew her into the room. She walked slowly around the sofa and coffee table until she was standing in front of him. She waited until he looked up at her, his pale blue eyes impatient at first for an explanation for her presence, then merely curious when she didn't say anything.

"Could I have a bite of that?" she finally asked, knowing that if she got a little food into her stomach, she could better control this awkward situation.

Jay reached into the brown paper sack at his elbow and pulled out two small white cartons. "I got a double order, so help yourself. I'm not as hungry as I thought."

Halley sank to her knees and tore into both cartons. She was too ravenous to go to the kitchen and find a plate and a fork. She unwrapped the chopsticks Jay had opted to ignore and began stuffing alternate bites of beef and fried rice into her mouth, right from the cartons. She kept up a breakneck pace for several minutes, until the clawing emptiness in her stomach began to ease. When she paused and glanced up, Jay was staring at her, looking frankly shocked.

"Halley, what is wrong with you?" he demanded.

She pushed the food cartons away and leaned back on the heels of her hands. "I was hungry," she said, her eyes downcast. "I haven't eaten since... I don't know, but it's been awhile.'

Hungry? Halley, whose table manners were normally Emily Post-perfect, had wolfed down that food like Conan the Barbarian. Again Jay was confronted with the certainty that something was radically out of kilter with her, beyond just the stress of traveling or anxiety over the divorce.

"Halley, what's wrong?" he asked again, more softly this time.

She shrugged off his concern. "A lot of things are wrong. The most significant thing is that I'm still here, and so are my boxes."

"I noticed." He propped his chin in his hand and waited patiently for her to continue.

She pushed herself off the floor and began pacing the small room, made smaller by the ceiling-high stacks of cartons. "Well, it's like this," she began, sounding decidedly shaken. "I arrived home from Europe this morning to discover that Harold Dempsey ripped me off."

"How? Don't tell me your paragon of efficiency has been doing a little creative accounting."

"Worse than that, I'm afraid. He cleaned me out and disappeared. Naturally, as busy as he's been bankrupting me, he didn't have time to get my boxes moved into the new apartment. So..." She shrugged. "Here I am."

Jay was silent for a long moment. "You're kidding, right?" Even before she shook her head, he knew she wasn't. "You mean that balding, middle-aged fussbudget with the bow tie is an embezzler?"

"Looks that way." She studied her nails. Her peach-colored polish was chipped in a couple of places, Jay noticed. The situation must be critical for her to allow that.

"Are you... will you have to declare bankruptcy?" Jay asked cautiously.

Halley's spine stiffened. "Certainly not," she answered fiercely. "I will not allow anyone to destroy my company. Kathryn and I made a list of everyone the agency owes. I called them all and explained the situation. Anyone who wouldn't give me a little time, I paid out of my personal account. The bank is going to arrange for a small line of credit against my accounts receivable, too, and Kathryn's been busy with collections. The doors will stay open." But with the end of her speech, she seemed to deflate again. "Of course, I only have seven dollars and fifty-three cents left in my personal account...." she said in a much smaller voice.

"I don't know what to say." He wanted to touch her, comfort her somehow, but he didn't know where to start. Halley had a habit of closing herself off when she was troubled or hurting. He had never been able to breach those barriers when she erected them.

"You don't have to say anything," she replied. "It's not your problem, especially not now. In fact, I wouldn't burden you with any of this, except that... I need to stay here tonight. To put it bluntly, I'm too broke and too exhausted to make other arrangements. I promise to be out tomorrow, if you'll just let me stay the night."

She made the request matter-of-factly enough, but Jay wasn't fooled. Her voice carried an edge of desperation. He watched helplessly as Halley's composure wavered, then abandoned her completely. She turned away from him quickly, but not before he saw the glint of moisture in her eyes.

The tears alarmed him. The only other time he'd seen her cry was the night they'd decided to divorce, and even then she hadn't given him the opportunity to react. She had raced out the door and disappeared for several hours, and when she'd returned, she'd been dry-eyed and calm.

She showed no signs of escaping now.

Still, he stifled the urge to go to her and pull her to him, to let her cry on his shoulder. For one thing, if he tried it she was likely to lash out at him like a wounded lioness. She was nothing if not proud.

"I guess you can stay here," he said, careful not to make it sound like a kind gesture. She would sooner sleep on the street than admit that she needed anything from him. But Jay could see her need, and the knowledge that it existed filled him with something warm and bright.

After a minute or so Halley turned again to face him, all signs of tears having disappeared. "I'm okay now," she mumbled. "Sorry. I didn't mean to fall apart on you."

"I wouldn't exactly call what you did 'falling apart.' But if you ever do feel like crying, Halley, I've got nice big shoulders, perfect for the job."

"I know you do," she agreed, almost wistfully, but when she continued, her manner was no-nonsense. "Just the same, I won't be needing them. I'm a big girl. I'll handle this like an adult."

"Adults are allowed to cry once in a while."

"I don't like to cry." She seemed irritated now, but more with herself than with him. "It's so . . . weak," she added.

"God forbid. Wouldn't want anyone to think you're a wimp, right?" He couldn't prevent a touch of bitterness from seeping into his voice. "I guess it's against your code of honor to accept comfort or sympathy, either, particularly from your husband . . . ex-husband, I mean.''

She glared at him, her aqua-blue eyes gleaming a warning.

"All right, that was a cheap shot," he admitted. "There's no point in rehashing old arguments. The shoulders are here if you change your mind, okay?''

She softened almost imperceptibly. "Thank you, but . . . just thank you, I guess.''

"And don't worry about having everything moved out by tomorrow. I'm sure you have enough to keep you busy for the time being, so don't feel you have to make moving your top priority. A few more days doesn't matter.''

"Thanks, but I'd feel better getting it taken care of tomorrow.''

"Fine." The word came out a little more clipped than he intended. Why did she find it so difficult to accept a simple offer of kindness from him?

"I'll sleep in the spare room, on the fold-out bed.''

"Fine," he repeated, turning away before he said something he'd regret. He moved to the wood-burning stove and added another log. By the time he was finished, she was gone, and he could hear the shower running. He retrieved her suitcases from the entry hall and carried them into the spare room, wondering why he bothered with the small gesture.

Halley awoke before sunrise the next morning, disoriented until her eyes adjusted to the darkness. Then she relaxed as she recognized the familiar exposed brick of her townhouse. Reflexively she reached a hand out to touch Jay. When she grasped only empty space, she remembered how and why she'd come to sleep on the lumpy sofa bed, and her heart sank in disappointment, like dozens of other mornings.

She stretched and yawned, sitting up resignedly. At least she'd managed to sleep soundly. Maybe today she would be better equipped to face the world than she had been yesterday.

With a grimace she recalled the tearful, confused woman who'd stood in that living room last night, practically begging Jay to let her stay here. The sound of her own voice had triggered uncomfortable childhood memories, memories of another woman who always had to ask, and sometimes beg, for something as simple as a new dress or use of the family car.

As she'd experienced the brief déjà vu, she'd been half afraid that Jay might gloat over her failure, that he might deny her request for a place to sleep. But then the premonition had passed, unfulfilled, and she realized she'd had nothing to fear. Despite all the difficulties they'd had during their marriage, despite all the bitterness that had come between them, Jay was simply too compassionate to ignore someone else's plight—even hers. He was nothing like her father. And luckily, she was nothing like her mother, either.

She took a quick shower and applied her makeup, then brushed her tangled hair, amazed she'd gone to bed in such a state. With nimble fingers she twisted the long strands into a French braid as she returned from the bathroom to the bedroom, wondering what she could wear that wasn't unbearably wrinkled. After a moment's debate, she selected a full, bias-cut skirt in black-and-white houndstooth check wool and a matching fitted top. Black hose and spectator pumps finished the outfit.

Feeling more in control now that she was well-groomed, she went to the kitchen and started the coffee. Idly she opened the refrigerator and, seeing the meager contents, rolled her eyes. What was Jay living on? Probably nothing but Chinese food, she decided. Neither of them had ever had much time or inclination to cook in recent years, but at least she'd kept the refrigerator stocked with something they could snack on, like cold cuts and raw vegetables.

Reluctantly she reached for one of the eggs. Normally she was not a breakfast person, but since she didn't know where her next meal was coming from, she decided to indulge in a little cholesterol. In the absence of butter or margarine, she coated a skillet with nonstick spray and set it on the stove to heat.

She'd just cracked the egg and dropped it into the pan when she heard the bedroom door open. *Rats*. She had hoped to get out of here before Jay was up. She'd been so stressed last night she hadn't had a chance to get nervous about facing him. Now her skittering nerves were treating her to a flamenco dance.

She turned her head just enough that she could peek over her shoulder and through the doorway. He was advancing through the living room and toward the kitchen at his usual morning-stumble pace, and wearing his usual morning attire—a skimpy pair of white gym shorts and nothing else.

Her breath quickened at the sight of so much well-sculpted body. She and Jay might have grown incompatible in many areas, but on a physical basis they'd never had a problem. She could not remain unaffected by the sight of him in such a state of undress, looking primal and all male.

She distracted herself by searching for a spatula as he entered the kitchen. Unexpectedly she felt a possessive hand at her waist and a warm, lingering kiss at the vulnerable nape of her neck.

"Morning, sweetheart," he said as he reached around her to get a coffee mug out of the cabinet.

Halley was shocked speechless. Jay hadn't so much as touched her since the night they'd agreed their marriage was a hopeless cause. That had been almost three months ago, and her body obviously knew it had been deprived, because that one light touch of lips to skin sent a sizzle all the way down to her toes.

She whirled around, intent on giving him a piece of her mind about his cavalier kiss, when she realized he wasn't fully awake. He'd managed to slosh some coffee from the pot into the mug, but now he was leaning against the counter, the cup in his hand suspended halfway to his mouth, his eyelids drooping.

Halley rescued the coffee before it spilled.

"Huh?" Jay said when she took the mug from his hand.

"Wake up, Casanova." She patted his stubbly cheek. "Take a few swigs of that coffee and get your bearings. Then I think you might want to put on some clothes before you catch pneumonia." She placed the mug back in his hands and turned around to flip the egg.

The silence behind her was deafening. What was he thinking?

When the egg was on a plate and the stove turned off, she chanced another look at him. He was staring at her over the rim of his coffee mug, his expression unreadable.

"Sorry, Halley," he finally managed. "You know how I am first thing in the morning."

Boy, did she. Drowsy and amorous pretty well summed it up. She'd lost count of the number of mornings he'd waylaid her, after she was already dressed, and coaxed her back into bed simply because he was damnably persistent and irresistibly touchable.

"I guess for a minute or two I forgot we were divorced," he added.

"I understand." She briskly carried her plate to the breakfast bar that separated kitchen from living room, aware of his eyes following her. Was he, too, remembering those glorious morning romps? The thought that he might be put a quiver in her stomach. Suddenly she had no appetite for breakfast, but she forced herself to eat it anyway. She was sure she needed the protein.

Silently Jay left the room. By the time she'd finished eating and rinsed her plate in the sink, he had showered and reappeared, dressed in a pair of stone-washed jeans and a royal blue sweatshirt. The jeans hugged his thighs in a way that made Halley again think of things she shouldn't, and she silently chided herself for being so vulnerable to Jay's uncompromising good looks.

"Before I go," he said, pulling on a pair of boots, "is there anything I can do to help? Anything you need?"

She almost asked him for taxi fare to her office, then resisted at the last minute. Begging for little bits of money here and there—that was something her mother did. "No, thanks. I do appreciate your letting me stay here last night, though."

"It was no big sacrifice." The house was quiet as he shrugged into his down jacket. "Well," he finally said, "I guess you'll be moved by the time I get home tonight."

"Uh-huh."

"Guess this is really goodbye, then." He smiled self-consciously, and Halley's heart wrenched. "We were both too mad at each other before to really say it," he added.

"Uh-huh." She swallowed, her mouth suddenly dry.

He held out his hand to her. "Goodbye, Halley. I hope everything works out for you."

"Yeah, you too." Their hands met. Jay grasped hers tightly for a moment, then abruptly released her as if the contact were uncomfortable.

After he had disappeared out the front door, Halley was left staring after him, trying to crawl out from under the shroud of sadness that had fallen over her. She shook herself after a few moments, forcing herself to get a grip on reality. She hadn't expected to see Jay again at all, so why should a formal goodbye make her feel so desolate?

She returned her attention to more immediate problems. First she should call her new apartment manager and make arrangements for getting a key. Then she would have to find a moving company that would charge something less than the national debt. And finally, she thought with distaste, she'd have to walk down the street to the bank and get a cash advance on her credit card from the automatic teller machine. She fervently hoped she hadn't already gone over her credit limit.

She pulled a business card out of her purse and picked up the kitchen phone, then dialed the number for her apartment manager. After six rings a scratchy-voiced man finally answered. Halley had obviously pulled Mr. Baxter out of bed.

She introduced herself and explained what she needed.

An ominous silence greeted her request, followed by a nervous throat-clearing.

"Is there a problem, Mr. Baxter?" she asked.

"Ms. Jernigan, your rental contract stated that you were to take possession and pay your first month's rent three days ago."

"Yes, but as I explained, I was unavoidably detained in Europe," Halley replied, sensing trouble.

"Well, I'm sorry about that, but your omission has rendered the contract null and void." The man was either a lawyer, or he'd been well coached by one. What was he trying to do, gouge her for a higher rent?

"How can I reinstate the contract?" she asked patiently.

"You can't. I already rented your apartment to someone else. They moved in yesterday. Naturally, your security deposit will be refunded within fourteen days."

A tight ball of panic started unraveling in the pit of her stomach. "Mr. Baxter, this just can't be!"

"I'm sorry, lady, but it is. Now I still have the other apartment available—"

"I can't *afford* the penthouse," she said. If the truth be known, she couldn't even afford the modest one-bedroom apartment she'd chosen—at least, not now.

"Then I guess we've finished our business. Good day, Ms. Jernigan."

"Wait, I—" He hung up.

Halley slammed the receiver onto the phone with enough force to shatter an eardrum, *if* anyone had still been listening. Now what was she going to do?

In a way this turn of events was a blessing, she supposed. Now she could find a less expensive place to live. But with all her money tied up in that deposit for the next two weeks, how could she scrape together enough to secure another apartment?

As she was pondering her most recent dilemma, the phone rang. She jumped, then picked it up, hoping that Mr. Baxter had changed his mind. "Hello?"

"Halley, I'm glad I caught you." It was Kathryn. "I know you're probably still fighting jet lag, but I just got a call from TNT Records. They're scouring the city for models for a big-budget video. A rep is coming over this morning to look through the composites, and I thought you might want to be here."

"You bet I do. Thanks. I'm on my way."

This was just the break she needed, Halley thought as she pushed her arms into the sleeves of her fox. If she had time, she'd find out what kind of models TNT was looking for, then arrange to have a few of her best prospects on hand with their books.

Now, how to get to the office? She dug through the bottom of her purse, locating only a couple of dollars in change and a bonus of some French francs. No time to visit the bank. A taxi was an extravagance anyway, given her circumstances. She'd have to reacquaint herself with the subway.

Two

By lunchtime Halley had retreated to her corner office, with its opulent white-on-white decor and its winter-weary plants. She hadn't wasted time watering or trimming the ferns, as she normally would after returning from a trip. There was too much to be done, and the man from TNT Records had already blown away her whole morning.

She had just gotten off the phone with a Mr. Abrams of the FBI, who had asked her endless, tedious questions about Harold Dempsey. No clue to the bookkeeper's whereabouts had been found, though Abrams had scrutinized the passenger list of every flight leaving the country. Harold's picture had been circulated among ticket agents and flight attendants, all to no avail.

"If he did leave the country, he was clever about it," Abrams had said. Halley had stifled a half-hysterical giggle as she'd pictured the prim and proper Harold hanging out on one of those wild, topless beaches in South America.

"But we think he might be laying low until the heat's off. If you had to guess, where do you think he might hide?"

Halley had been at a loss. Harold had never spoken of family or close friends. "I'm afraid I just wasn't very intimate with Mr. Dempsey," she'd explained. "He was an excellent employee until this happened, devoted strictly to his work. He never offered personal information, and I never asked for it."

Maybe that's why she'd told Harold, and no one else, about her divorce, she mused as Abrams paused, probably so he could take notes. Their relationship had been so impersonal that divulging her secret to him had been something like confessing to a priest. She'd known he wouldn't tell anyone, because he didn't gossip. His reaction had been cautiously, coolly concerned—nothing that would encourage further confidences.

Mr. Abrams had thanked Halley and hung up. She had no sooner started to arrange her afternoon responsibilities when Kathryn buzzed her again.

"*She's* here," Kathryn hissed.

Halley didn't have to ask who *she* was—Maureen Argent, an acquaintance of Harold's who happened to be a rather well-known model. Maureen had had a row with her own agent, and since Harold, who was infatuated with her, had all but promised that Halley would represent her, the woman had been making a pest of herself.

Halley had already decided she would never represent Maureen. It wasn't that Maureen wasn't beautiful—she was, despite her advancing age. In fact, she was still in high demand as a runway model. But she was undependable, and her growing reputation as "difficult" would have reflected badly on the Mystique Agency. If there was one quality Halley demanded of her models, it was professionalism. Maureen just wouldn't have fit in. What was more, Maureen took part in a dissipating life-style with a sleazy crowd Halley took great pains to avoid.

"What does she want?" Halley asked Kathryn.

"She says she has a lunch appointment with you."

"Darn, I thought that was next week." Halley glanced at her calendar. "It *is* next week. Oh, never mind. Tell her I'll be up front in a minute."

Halley hung up the phone and shoved her feet into her pumps. Dealing with Maureen's delicate ego was the last thing she needed to do right now. She stood just as Maureen burst through her office door.

"Darling, how are you!" The tall, painfully thin woman greeted Halley with a conservative hug. The familiarity was overdone, given that they knew each other only slightly. "I didn't think you'd mind if I just came on back. Are you ready for some lunch?" She looked fashion-plate perfect, as always.

Secretly Halley wondered when Maureen's excesses would catch up with her looks. "Maureen, our appointment isn't till next week," Halley scolded mildly.

"You don't say?" Maureen made a production out of extracting a tiny leather-bound appointment book from her lizard-skin bag. She pursed her plum-glossed lips. "My goodness, you're absolutely correct. How silly of me!"

"And I'm up to my ears in paperwork . . ." Halley tried to usher her toward the door.

"Oh, it's no problem, sweetie. I could do with skipping lunch today anyway, if the bathroom scales are any judge. I'll go shopping. Is Harold in?" she asked, raising one finely arched brow in a question mark. "He's been promising to take a look at my year-end financial statement for ages. I haven't been able to catch him at home, so I thought I'd try and corner him here."

"Harold is . . . out of town," Halley improvised, edging Maureen out her office door and toward the foyer.

"I see." Maureen gave a well-practiced pout, but she took the hint and headed for the exit. "I want to hear all about your trip." She left in a flourish of expensive perfume that made Halley sneeze.

"Oh, Lord, she's so awful," Kathryn said with a grimace. "How can you stand her?"

"She's not awful," Halley objected. "That unique style of hers earns her a bundle on the runway. She's simply not this agency's cup of tea."

"What did you tell her about Harold?" Kathryn asked.

"As little as possible. She's going to be a problem, though. Eventually she'll have to know the truth, but I'd rather she didn't until the agency is back on its feet. She's a bit of a gossip, and if word gets out that we're in financial trouble it could hurt us more than we're already hurting."

Kathryn nodded solemnly.

The rest of Halley's day was even more hectic. She rushed from the conference room to a tutoring session with a seventeen-year-old she'd just taken on, instructing her in makeup application and hairstyling. She had to stall two other models who wanted their checks for previous work—something she'd never had to do before. After that, her publicity director demanded a raise. The woman was lucky she didn't get fired on the spot, considering the mood Halley was in.

It was almost four o'clock before she found time to eat, and though she was famished, she had to settle for a cup of raspberry yogurt from the staff kitchen refrigerator. As she sat wearily in a hard plastic chair, reminding herself to eat slowly and calm down, she was forced to admit that she wasn't going to find an apartment today—or tomorrow, or the next day for that matter unless a miracle came to her aid.

She hoped Jay would keep an open mind.

* * *

For the second consecutive night Jay slogged home in the snow after dark, though at least he had boots this time. Again he dreaded entering the house and the prospect of facing the emptiness. And again he was surprised when he opened the front door, though this surprise was much more to his liking than tripping over a suitcase. He was greeted by the scent of oregano and garlic and spicy tomatoes.

"Is that you, Jay?" Her voice drifted from the kitchen.

Jay glanced into the living room before answering. The boxes seemed to have taken root. Yesterday he'd been irritated by their presence, but today he was merely curious—and a little amused that Halley was having such a difficult time accomplishing her move. Normally when she made up her mind to do something, it got done one way or another.

"It's me," he called out as he removed his jacket and boots. He followed the mouth-watering scent to the kitchen, where he found Halley, leaning over a saucepan and stirring purposefully. She still wore her proper dress-for-success clothes, except that her feet were encased in pink bunny slippers. "I thought maybe I was having an olfactory hallucination," he said. "But you're really cooking—spaghetti sauce?"

"Uh-huh."

He glanced around for a can or a jar and saw none. "You can make homemade spaghetti sauce?"

She didn't look up at him. "One of my many untapped talents."

"Any particular reason for this sudden bout of domesticity?" he asked, sensing subterfuge.

She sighed, finally glancing up. "I just had this sudden urge to cook—no, that's not quite the truth. This is a bribe."

"Does this have anything to do with the fact that your boxes are still stacked in the living room?" He peeked into the oven. A foil-wrapped loaf of garlic bread was warming on the top rack. She was going the whole nine yards.

"As a matter of fact, it does," she answered, setting down her spoon and facing him squarely. "I'm in real trouble financially, Jay. I don't have an apartment to move into, and my deposit is tied up for the next two weeks. The agency is barely hanging on, so I can't depend on any income from that source for a while. This spaghetti dinner represents the better part of the last twenty dollar cash advance I could squeeze out of my overextended credit cards."

"I see." He felt disappointed. What had he expected her to say—that she'd experienced an overwhelming need to share a real home-cooked dinner with him, for a change? "You didn't have to go to all this trouble. If it's just a matter of borrowing some money—"

"No! I don't want your money."

Of course she didn't. When she was just starting the agency, she wouldn't allow him to finance even a small part of it—not as a gift, a loan, or a legitimate investment. In truth, she hadn't really needed his money then. Though she'd had her ups and downs, the agency had done quite well. But her refusing his help had rankled him then, as it did now. "What is it you want, then?"

"I need to stay here awhile—not long, a week or two at the most. Just until I can pull something together."

"You don't have to—"

"Let me finish. Regardless of what you say, I know this is an imposition. Awkward, at best. So I'm prepared to do something in return."

Jay's mind reeled with interesting possibilities. "And that is?"

"I'll cook dinner for you every night. I know how much you love home-cooked meals—I mean, you used to practically beg me to take you home to my mom's so she could cook for you. Well, I can cook just about everything she does. I'll make you whatever you want if you pay for the groceries..." She finally ran out of wind.

Jay's jaw had dropped a good three inches. "You didn't cook even when we were married, unless it came out of a box."

"This has nothing to do with when we were married," she countered. "This is a simple business proposition—your spare bedroom for my cooking services. Is it a deal?"

He'd have given her the bedroom for nothing. Hell, just yesterday he was anxious to have her gone, to sever the last ties once and for all and be done with it. But something had changed in the last twenty-four hours. If he were honest with himself, he'd admit that the prospect of her living here was suddenly quite palatable—exciting, even.

"I'll do your laundry, too," she added when he didn't answer right away.

A live-in cook and laundress, every man's fantasy—except his, not with Halley. Although he'd enjoyed those few occasions when she'd prepared a special dinner for him, because she'd done it in such an obvious effort to please him, he'd never wanted or expected her to be his maid. And he certainly wouldn't enjoy eating the meals she prepared if he thought for one minute that she viewed cooking as a chore or an obligation.

"You can stay here as long as you need to," he finally answered. "But no cooking and no laundry. When would you find the time?"

"I'll make the time. Anyway, I insist. I have to do something to repay you."

"No, you don't," he said firmly. "You aren't obligated to me in any way."

She eyed him thoughtfully for a few moments. "Is it all right if I cook for myself?"

She was cagey, he thought, suppressing a grin. No matter what he said or did, she was going to cook. And once the food was on the table, she knew he wouldn't turn it down. It also occurred to him that if he didn't provide groceries, she might not eat at all, not if she was as strapped as she claimed.

"Yes, you can cook for yourself." He reached into his back pocket and pulled out his wallet, then withdrew a handful of bills and tucked them under the cookie jar on top of the refrigerator. "That's for groceries and whatnot," he said, leaving Halley's options open. If she needed panty hose or taxi fare, he hoped she'd have the sense to use the money. But he knew better than to make the offer aloud.

With that issue as settled as it was going to get, Halley served up the spaghetti, salad, and crisp garlic bread while Jay opened a bottle of jug wine and poured some into two glasses.

They ate at the bar, rather than in the formal confines of the dining room. Gradually they relaxed as the level of wine moved down the side of the jug, and their conversation drifted naturally to familiar, impersonal subjects. Halley related the highlights of her European trip, and Jay told her about his new client, an avant-garde jeweler who had given him carte blanche to shoot the unusual baubles any way he wanted.

"Sounds like just the sort of job you love," Halley said. "I don't suppose you need any models?"

She wouldn't ask for favors, Jay thought, but she wasn't above drumming up some legitimate business. "I wish modeling fees were in the budget, but they aren't."

"Oh, well, can't blame me for asking. Say, though, I've got a new girl who's trying to build up her book," Halley suggested. "She'll work gratis."

"And she probably looks all of eighteen."

"Seventeen, actually. You envision someone more mature for this jewelry, is that it?"

"Mature, exotic, and sophisticated—someone along your lines would be perfect."

She laughed. "I'm more than mature. I'm over the hill by modeling standards. I reached my peak at age twenty-four, remember? I haven't been in front of a camera since I opened the agency."

"But you could be, if you wanted. You're hardly over the hill at twenty-nine. You haven't lost a thing, trust me." He hadn't meant the comment to come out sounding suggestive, but it had.

Halley froze for a moment, her fork suspended halfway to her mouth. She looked up quickly, as if to gauge his meaning, then back down. She ate the bite of spaghetti, chewing it thoroughly before responding.

"That's how I could pay you back," she said quietly.

"What? Halley, I didn't mean it like that. I wasn't hinting around. I'm perfectly happy to do the jewelry shoot without models."

"No, really," she persisted. "We could do one shoot, in the evening when it wouldn't interfere with other business. That would be a perfect way for me to pay you back."

"And I keep telling you, you don't owe me."

"It would make me feel so much better, though," she argued. "We can do some really fun stuff that'll make your client turn cartwheels. And you'll have some fashion shots for your portfolio—you mentioned that you wanted to update it."

"I'll talk to the client and see if he's interested," Jay said, though his noncommittal reply belied his tumultuous feelings on the subject. A million memories chased each other through his mind, memories of other times he'd photographed Halley. He saw fleeting images of her—serious, sexy, innocent, laughing. But eventually the memories settled down to something he hadn't recalled in a long time—the day they'd met. She was just getting into serious modeling then, and her agent had sent her to Jay's studio for some portfolio shots.

He'd immediately decided she was the most naturally sexy woman he'd ever photographed. Though he was proud of his businesslike detachment on the rare occasions when he worked with female models, he'd blown it with Halley. As he'd focused on her hands, her legs, the curve of her neck, her moist lips, he'd wanted her with an intensity that had been new to him. Only her supposed age—eighteen—had prevented him from crossing the line of professional ethics and acting on his desires.

As they'd chatted during the shoot, she'd inadvertently revealed a lot about herself—things that had only served to attract him further. She was a spunky girl from a small town in Pennsylvania who was fiercely determined to take New York by storm—and determined to do it on her own. Though there were plenty of men out there who would have "sponsored" her career, Halley would have none of it. Jay had admired her strength, her ethics, her independence.

But he'd had to remind himself—several times—that she was only a child.

A few days later when she'd dropped by the studio to pick up the prints, she'd let it slip that she was actually twenty-two—too old to be starting out as a New York model. Unbearably relieved to discover she was a responsible adult, he'd promised to keep her secret if she'd have dinner with him. Six months later they'd been married.

Though that burning independent streak of Halley's had once drawn Jay like a moth to a flame, he'd assumed that it sprang from need—her need to escape her middle-class, small-town roots and to have some financial security. From what he understood, her growing-up years had been pretty austere at times, though she talked little about her past. But he'd thought that once she had *him* to lean on, she wouldn't need to be so all-fired proud. He'd expected her to mellow out. But if anything, she had become even more determined to go it alone.

Instead of relaxing and enjoying her modeling career, she'd worked herself hard, saving every penny, something that had baffled Jay given that he was earning a very comfortable living for the two of them. When she'd announced that she was quitting modeling to start her own agency, it had been a shock. How could a twenty-four-year-old woman with no education and no business experience even consider such a thing? But she wanted it with such a passion that Jay hadn't had the heart to tell her her venture was doomed—or so he thought.

From that moment on she'd never posed in front of a camera, his or anyone else's. That's why he was now so surprised by her sudden turnabout.

The other thought that occurred to Jay, as he stared into his wine, was that just the prospect of photographing her made him excited. He was suddenly plagued by libidinous thoughts of Halley, his ex-wife, that were no longer his privilege. He shifted uncomfortably in his chair and took a sip of the wine, hoping to clear his mind.

He hadn't felt such an acute lust for Halley in a long, long time. He knew this sudden desire was somehow tied to the fact that she was in dire straits, and that disturbed him. He didn't examine that tie too closely, however. He was sure he'd thought through every angle of their relationship, yet suddenly he suspected that he might have missed something important.

Jay whistled tunelessly as he stood on a ladder, hanging the hand-painted fabric that would serve as a backdrop for the jewelry shoot. With great care he draped the soft, muted cotton into gentle pleats and folds. The color would show off Halley and the sparkling gems to perfection.

His whistling had changed to humming by the time Peg emerged from the darkroom with a handful of her latest efforts, a dozen or so photos of forklift parts.

"You're certainly in a cheerful mood for a cold, gray afternoon," she commented as she laid the prints out on a table in a black-and-white patchwork design. "Would you take a look at these when you get a chance?"

"I'm not so much cheerful as nervous," Jay admitted, giving the backdrop one final pat before climbing off the ladder. He strolled over to the table and began to examine the photographs.

"About the jewelry?" Peg asked. "Why? You've shot that kind of thing before. And the collection is gorgeous." She nodded toward a table, where Jay had laid out the gold and gemstone trinkets in compatible groupings.

"The jewelry is no problem. It's the model I'm worried about."

"You didn't tell me you'd hired a model." She pointed to one of the forklift photos. "Did I get enough contrast here?"

Jay took a closer look at the print she indicated. "Looks fine to me. And I didn't hire a model. She's offering her services gratis."

"Oh, no, don't tell me—the jeweler's wife?"

"Nope. My wife. Ex-wife, that is."

"Halley?" Peg's eyes grew even wider than usual.

"Only ex-wife I have."

"Wait a minute, Jay. For weeks you moped around because she was supposedly out of your life. What happened?" Before Jay could reply, Peg offered him a hopeful smile. "A reconciliation?"

"No, nothing like that," Jay answered hastily. "But things haven't turned out quite the way they were supposed to. Halley's had some problems getting moved out, and—"

"You mean she's still *living* with you?" Peg cut in.

"Well, yeah. Just for a few days. The reasons aren't important," he went on, unwilling to discuss Halley's financial crisis, even with someone he trusted as completely as Peg. "What's important is for you to stick around for this shoot. I, um, might need your advice."

"My advice? Hah!" She folded her arms over her ample bosom and tilted her chin down, peering skeptically at Jay over the rims of her glasses. "That'll be the day when you listen to my advice, Swede. What's the real reason you want me to hang around? You think you need a bodyguard or something?"

"Or something. Never mind why, will you do it?"

She shrugged. "Sure. I have to stay and finish these forklift pictures anyway."

Jay grinned his thanks just as he heard the front door slam. "Hello? Jay?"

"Come on back, Halley," he called to her. "I'm almost ready for you." And that, he decided, was an unfortunately accurate choice of words. He had been ready for her since this morning, when he'd accidentally caught a glimpse of her coming out of her bedroom in a silky silver nightgown that clung to her as if it were wet. She'd been on his mind all day, first as he'd sketched out ideas for several possible shots, then later as he'd prepared the set.

Now she was here, conjured from a dream. She strolled across the squeaky warehouse floor, a makeup case in one hand, holding a garment bag slung over her shoulder with the other. She wore a pair of faded jeans tucked into her leather mukluks, and a bulky green sweater. It occurred to Jay that he had seldom seen her dressed so casually. He liked it.

"Since I was walking over here I decided to get comfortable," she said, guessing his thoughts.

"You walked in this weather? Why didn't you take a—" He stopped himself before completing the thought, already knowing the answer. She didn't have the money for a cab. "Peg or I could have picked you up," he finished lamely.

"Oh, I wanted to walk," she said. "I needed the time to clear my head—you know, to forget about business. Now, what do you want me to wear?" She set down the makeup case and zipped open the garment bag, revealing half a dozen blouses in various styles and shades, from a slinky black halter to a ruffled, long-sleeved number in peach satin. "I just assumed we're shooting from the waist up," she added.

"For the most part," he answered, his eye immediately drawn to the low-cut halter, picturing Halley in it. As enticing as she would look, he dismissed it. Customers wouldn't even notice the jewelry if it had to compete with Halley in *that*. Instead he decided to start with a simple silk blouse that buttoned up the back. The low, rounded neckline would reveal just enough throat, he judged, and the deep forest green would accent Halley's dramatic coloring without overpowering the product.

"And my hair?" Halley asked.

"Wear it up, but not too severe. And use neutral tones for your makeup—understated, but elegant."

She gave him a salute. "You certainly know what you want. That's more than I get from most clients. I'll be back in a few minutes." She picked up her things and headed for the dressing room.

Peg sighed as Halley made her exit. "Why didn't she continue modeling? She could have made a fortune."

"That's a question I've asked myself often enough," he replied. "Sometimes I think that if she'd just stuck to modeling . . ." He stopped. What he was about to say was that if Halley had remained a model, they might never have gotten divorced. It was an odd thing to pop into his mind. It wasn't true, either.

"What were you going to say?" Peg asked, peering at him curiously.

He hedged. "If she had stuck to modeling, she might have done well, but she hasn't done too badly with the agency. She *did* make a fortune."

"You sound almost proud of her."

"Shouldn't I be?"

"Don't get defensive. It's just that before, you always seemed to make light of her business. You used to call it her hobby, remember?"

Jay winced. He did remember. "I thought once she found out how hard it was to run a business, she'd go back to what she was meant to do and be happy with it. I sure called that one wrong."

Peg gave him a sharp look. "What she was *meant* to do? Good heavens, I'd have divorced you, too."

"I didn't say I still felt that way. I know I was a little off base, but that doesn't have anything to do with why we got divorced."

But it did, he realized. Though he had encouraged Halley to open her agency, he'd had no real faith in her abilities. So he'd humored her, waiting for her to grow tired of her ridiculous venture and return to what she was good at— modeling. She had surprised the hell out of him when she started making money.

At that point he'd subtly withdrawn his moral support, and that's precisely when their troubles had begun.

This was something that bore further scrutiny, but not now. Now, he had to focus all of his attention on getting through this shoot.

Peg gave him a knowing look, then whisked by him imperiously to collect her photos on her way to the darkroom.

Halley emerged from the dressing room a very few minutes later, having transformed herself into a tempting seductress. "Is the hair okay?" she asked in a professional tone that quarreled with her unearthly visual image.

Perfect, he wanted to say. All of her was perfect, from her glossy mahogany hair to her moist, full lips to the soft denim that curved down her thigh and hugged her slim calves. "Fine," he replied, trying not to stare. "The jewelry is laid out on the table over there. Start with the grouping on the left."

She moved briskly in stocking feet toward the table. She was the picture of cool courtesy, and her polite detachment unnerved him, especially given his own inner turmoil. He'd like to think she was as nervous about this as he was.

"These are beautiful," she said, admiring the cabochon ruby ring on her long, slender hand. The huge central gem was surrounded by an asymmetrical grouping of emerald and diamond slivers. "But what in the world is this?" She held up two gold and emerald pieces, one larger than the other, connected by a shimmering chain.

"The smaller one is an earring," Jay answered, smiling at the most whimsical piece of the collection. "You pin the larger onto your blouse, like a brooch."

Halley tried it on, then inspected her image in a mirror on the wall. She shook her head and watched the chain sway to and fro. "Neat. Where can I buy one?"

"At a shop on the Upper East Side. For a cool ten grand, I believe."

She grimaced. "Not on my budget, I'm afraid, not unless I win the lottery. Are you ready to shoot?"

"All set. Just have a seat on the stool, center stage."

The jewelry looked good on her, Jay decided as he focused the camera. But then, he'd known it would. Whatever Halley put on, she wore with style. The gems had become imbued with her personal flair the moment they'd touched her skin.

"Give me a three-quarter profile," he directed. "Good. Bring your knee up and rest your elbow there. Don't worry, the jeans won't show. Now bring your hand to your chin...."

Working with Halley was a delight, Jay thought, in terms of efficiency and sensuality. She seemed to read his mind, knowing exactly the angle, the tilt of her chin, the direction of her gaze, so that little time was lost in making adjustments, and the shots were accomplished quickly. At the same time it was sheer pleasure to watch her—the contours of her smooth face as light and shadow played over it, the reddish highlights that gleamed from her dark, silky hair, the rise and fall of her small, perfect breasts as she breathed.

She wore nothing under the thin blouse, Jay judged with a practiced eye. The silk clung too smoothly to be covering anything but skin.

Whenever she looked directly at the camera with her expressive aqua eyes, Jay was seized by uncomfortable prickles of awareness. Though he knew on an intellectual level that Halley's smoldering gaze was strictly for the camera's benefit, it sent misleading signals to the rest of him. She used to look at *him* that way, and when she did, it could mean only one thing. Like a Pavlov dog, his body responded to that look.

He was glad he'd asked Peg to stay. She remained nearby, offering a suggestion here and there, powdering Halley's nose and chin when they became shiny under the hot lights, and making small adjustments to her hair and clothing per Jay's directions. Not only was Peg helpful, but her presence prevented him from saying—or doing—anything foolish.

The first four sets of shots were finished in record time. Jay mentally congratulated himself—only one set to go, and so far he'd managed to stay a safe distance from his alluring model. That didn't mean he wasn't uncomfortably aroused. In fact, he felt a distinct urge to run outside and dump a handful of snow down his jeans.

As Halley removed the bracelet and necklace they'd just shot, Peg glanced at her Mickey Mouse watch. "My film is dry by now," she announced to Jay. "This is all very glamorous, but the forklift parts are calling me." She started for the darkroom. "Yell if you need anything."

"Uh, wait, Peg..."

But she strolled away, unhearing, or perhaps merely ignoring him.

Halley didn't miss Peg's exit, either, and she quivered inside at the prospect of being alone with Jay under these circumstances. She'd felt his gaze through the entire shoot, caressing her as surely as she knew his hands could. There was something undeniably sensuous about a man focusing his attention so thoroughly on a woman, scrutinizing every curve and angle. Every model experienced at least a transient sexual pull toward her photographer, sooner or later. But when the man was Jay, a man Halley's body already ached for, the situation became much more intense.

Though his interest might be strictly professional, her body responded in a most unprofessional manner. When he coaxed her to move this way or that with a voice as smooth as vanilla, she heard a lover's voice, anxious and full of approval. Her nipples tightened beneath the silk blouse, and she struggled not to squirm.

Only one more shot to complete, though. She forced her attention to the final grouping of jewelry, drawing on what little reserve she had left. "Let's see. A tiara with a matching bracelet, right?" she asked, examining the stunning pieces, which featured diamonds and blue topaz.

"Close. The 'tiara' actually goes across your forehead."

"Like something Cleopatra would wear?" She experimented with the headpiece in front of the mirror.

"And the bracelet is for your ankle."

"My ankle? Oh." She looked down at her jeans. "Denim won't do, I bet."

"Can you roll one leg up?" Jay asked. "I just need your calf. Here, let me show you the sketch."

She peered at the drawing he gave her. "Interesting pose." The figure he'd sketched didn't appear to be wearing any clothes, though it was really too rough for Halley to be sure. Still, she understood the look Jay wanted, and she had no doubts that the resulting photos would be tasteful.

"What do you think?" Jay prompted.

"I can't roll these jeans up, they're too narrow at the ankle. But I think I know of something that might work." She handed the drawing back to him and retreated to the privacy of the dressing room, grateful for a brief respite from his intense nearness.

After allowing herself a few moments to fully collect herself, she looked around the room until she spotted what she remembered seeing earlier—a black strapless cocktail dress, hanging forlornly on a hook, forgotten by some model, no doubt, months or even years ago. Photographers sometimes had the oddest things lying about.

Quickly she stripped and donned the slinky dress, which turned out to be a bit snug, but it would do for Jay's purposes. She examined herself critically in the mirror, grinning as she realized she'd tucked the jeweled headpiece on top of her head like a crown. She looked ridiculous, like an overly mature prom queen.

Now she could laugh at her earlier qualms. Nothing was going to happen. Neither she nor Jay was likely to make a pass at the other, regardless of a little residual chemistry lurking between them. Their relationship was part of the past, and they were both resigned to that fact.

She expected Jay to laugh when he saw her in the ill-fitting dress. But his reaction was far from one of humor. Instead he stared as if she were strolling across the studio in a Calvin Klein original. His gaze was one of such frank interest, in fact, that she looked down at herself just to make sure she was indeed decently covered.

"Where on earth did you find that?" he asked, his eyes roaming irreverently over her body. Of course, he had to assess her costume to determine whether it was appropriate for the photograph. But she got the distinct impression that his thoughts centered on something more than cameras and lights.

"In the dressing room." She shrugged, immediately regretting the gesture as the bodice slipped downward. She tugged at it until it was again positioned correctly. Her former optimism faded. Peg was still nowhere to be seen, and the chemistry she'd thought of as "residual" seemed suddenly dangerous.

Three

———

"**W**ill the dress do?" Halley asked, moving toward the set where the light was better.

"If you can hike it above your knees, it'll be perfect. But lose the socks."

She looked down at her thick argyle socks peeking out from beneath her hem. The ridiculous sight of them, so incongruous, took the edge off her tension. She actually laughed.

Jay had moved a carpeted platform onto the set. When she was seated there, jewelry in place, socks removed, and dress hiked up to midthigh and tucked between her legs, she had serious doubts about this photo. "Jay, I feel distinctly *un*glamorous," she announced as he took some readings with the light meter. She sat sideways to the camera, feet on the platform, leaning forward over bent knees. "Are you sure this is going to work? Are you sure it's tasteful? I won't look naked, will I?"

"You *know* I wouldn't take a shot of you that wasn't tasteful."

"But will I look naked?" In her modeling days, Halley had adamantly refused to do any shots, tasteful or otherwise, that required disrobing. No ads for panty hose or body lotion. She'd even turned down an extremely lucrative national perfume campaign.

"I'll let you see the proof," Jay answered. "If you don't like it, we'll try something else."

Fair enough, she decided, though he hadn't answered her question.

When Jay moved to his position behind the camera, Halley dismissed all doubts so she could concentrate. No matter how easy it looked to an outsider, she considered modeling hard work, requiring intense muscular control and unwavering patience.

"You'll love this," he assured her a few minutes later, as he handed her the proof. "You look like a pagan goddess."

She wasn't sure she wanted to look like a pagan goddess, but nonetheless the photo impressed her. The shot was tight, focusing in on her bare legs, shoulders, and face. And she didn't look naked, though the effect was definitely provocative.

"I like it," she said, "but . . ."

"Too much skin? I know how you feel about that—"

"No, it's not that," she broke in hastily. "I think it's my hair. I should wear it down, if you want that 'pagan' look."

Jay agreed immediately. He watched, seemingly fascinated, as she removed one pin after another until the mass of her hair fell to her shoulders and below. His warm gaze brought back memories of those times she used to sit at her dressing table and brush her hair just for his pleasure, a prelude to lovemaking. Unconsciously she gave her head a shake, so that the curled ends of her hair teased her bare arms and back. She shivered despite the warm lights.

"Do I need to brush it?" she asked, her voice wavering.

"No, it looks great . . . beautiful." Jay sounded less than steady, too. He moved toward the camera, seeming to hide behind it, but Halley knew his eyes were on her, his full attention focused on her face, her body.

After a few shots, he decided her hair wasn't quite right after all. "There's a strand falling over your forehead that shouldn't be," he said.

She reached up to smooth her hair, finger-combing it away from her face. "How's that?"

He frowned. "Now there's a piece sticking up on top."

"I better go to the mirror."

"Wait, don't," he said, halting her before she could move. "I'm afraid we'll never get you back in the same position."

He came toward her, pulling a comb from his back pocket as he did. She sensed his reluctance, felt her own hesitation. He was going to touch her.

She closed her eyes and clenched her jaw as he toyed with the offending strands of hair, separating them, combing and smoothing until they behaved. Then he tidied the rest of her hair, working it around her ear just so, draping it over the curve of her shoulder and down her arm.

She wasn't sure just when his ministrations turned into caresses, but gradually she became aware of his fingers stroking her cheek. Her first reaction was outrage. He had no right to touch her like this. She wrenched her eyes open and pushed his hand away, glaring at him with all the anger she'd kept carefully banked over the past weeks. But she saw such torment in his face that her rage quickly melted, leaving an impossible rush of desire in its place.

"Oh, Jay," she said on a hopeless sigh, pulling his hand close again, laying her cheek against it. "I ought to slap you silly." The gentleness in her voice belied the harsh words.

"I know," he agreed, slipping his hand under her hair to the back of her neck. "I can be a real jerk sometimes."

She should push him away, she thought dazedly. All she had to do was voice a clear objection, and he would back off. But she couldn't seem to get the words past her lips, even when he leaned closer.

"Stop me before I cross the line," he pleaded in a throaty whisper.

"Too late, Jay." The words were scarcely out of her mouth before his lips touched hers, surprisingly shy at first, then increasingly firm and sure as her acceptance of the kiss became clear.

Her own response was hardly tentative; she drank in his attention as she would a tempting but forbidden brew. She felt as if she'd been denied his kiss for a lifetime, and no rational thought was going to interfere with the joy of the moment. Before she knew it, her arms were wrapped around his neck, holding him close as if he might try to escape her, and her fingers wound their way through his thick blond hair.

Her blood warmed with each passing second that he held her, coursing through her veins at record speeds, heating every part of her until she was sure she couldn't hold herself upright. Only Jay's hand at the back of her neck prevented her from slumping into a boneless heap.

His lips meandered away from hers, tracing a trail along her jawline and down her neck, pausing at the sensitive hollow of her throat to nuzzle and tease. She gasped, then sighed with pleasure as his hand took possession of her breast. Gone was any sign of shyness he'd shown only moments before. He kneaded her nipple through the thin material of her dress with practiced finesse, knowing from countless hours of lovemaking exactly how much pressure to exert.

The exquisite pleasure he brought filled her, sending shots of white heat into every fiber of her body.

She might not have noticed the groaning water pipes overhead, except that the intrusive sound broke Jay's concentration. His maddening caress slowed, and he lifted his head, breaking contact between his lips and the fullness of her breast where it overflowed from the snug dress.

"What is it?" she whispered, hating the world for intruding. But with the untimely intrusion came a measure of sanity. Slowly she released Jay as the full extent of her actions came into sharp focus.

"It's Peg. She's shutting things down in the darkroom. I can tell by the sound of the pipes." He pulled away from Halley then, but his eyes still held hers captive. He was so transparent, so obviously full of regret at what had just passed between them.

Halley looked away first, putting a hand to her forehead as she did. "I'm such a fool," she muttered.

"You should have stopped me."

"Right. Like it's so easy for me to push you away. About as easy as it is for an alcoholic to push away a drink."

"Come on, I'm not that irresistible." His attempt at lightness fell flat as an egg dropped on concrete.

"Don't you dare make a joke of this. We *divorced* each other, remember?" She swung her legs off the platform, then stood and went to the mirror to adjust her hair. "I'm only just now getting used to the idea. You had no right to come along and—"

"Don't you think I know that? I didn't mean for it to happen."

Halley wiped off her smeared lipstick with a tissue, giving herself a moment to cool off. "I guess neither one of us was thinking," she finally said. "I shouldn't be blaming you." She whirled around to face him with a menacing wag of her finger. "But next time I *will* slap you silly, I don't care who's fault it is. Have you got that?"

He nodded mutely, turning his attention to his camera.

"I'll need to fix my makeup before we continue," she said, once more adopting her professional persona.

"Let's call it a night, Halley. I have enough."

"But you said—"

"It was a little strand of hair across your forehead. The shots I took were good, plenty good enough."

"If you're sure?"

"I'm sure. Why don't you catch a ride home with Peg? I have a few things to take care of here."

"Okay." She was unutterably relieved that the ordeal was over.

Halley kicked a newspaper out of her way as she walked up the stairs toward the entrance of a brown brick apartment house in Chelsea. "Quaint," the classified ad had described it, which Halley had immediately translated to "old and rundown." But the rent was within her budget, and the neighborhood, though not terribly chic, appeared quiet and safe enough.

She'd stepped up her apartment search considerably since the photo session. It was imperative that she move away from Jay as soon as possible.

It could have turned out worse, she reminded herself. With a good night's sleep to separate them from their moment's madness, an air of normalcy had returned the morning after the shoot. Halley had made coffee, Jay had mixed up some orange juice, and they'd talked of trivialities just as if the kiss had never been.

But it had been, she acknowledged, and something indefinable had changed between them because of it. It was as though, once unleashed from Pandora's box, the passion that had flared so briefly now lurked somewhere nearby, ready to strike again during the first vulnerable moment. Desire seemed to prowl through Halley's veins, quietly stalking her, waiting for an unwary moment. She felt it rustle inside her at the oddest times—when Jay stirred the embers of the fire at night, staring into the stove lost in thought, or when he read the paper with his morning coffee, chuckling over his favorite political cartoon.

She had to get away from him and get on with her life. Enough of this torture.

The building had character, she decided as she pulled open the massive front door. No outer security lock, though. She paused in the foyer to coldly take stock of the aesthetics. The intricate tile floor, though cracked, gave the place a certain dignity. She took a sniff and wrinkled her nose at the strong odor of disinfectant. Someone kept the place clean, that was for sure.

She'd looked at her share of apartments over the past three days—a dozen at least. So far this one had the most promise. Given the scarcity of livable apartments in Manhattan, she considered herself lucky to find even a remotely suitable prospect that fit her budget.

The building manager, a paunchy, kind-faced man missing several teeth, ushered her into the upstairs one-bedroom unit. "It's a real bargain, yessir," he said right away. "Lots of space, big windows, high ceilings. The heat's paid, you know."

Halley tried to focus on the windows. But she saw peeling paint and worn carpet over a badly sloping floor.

"The kitchen's through here," the manager said, obviously sensing her dissatisfaction.

She followed him through a doorway, pleasantly surprised. The appliances were nothing fancy but they were fairly new, as the ad promised, and the porcelain sink had only one small chip to mar it.

The bathroom was a disaster, with rusted fixtures, a streaked mirror, and crumbling grout. Its saving grace was a huge, footed tub, which would afford Halley the long, steamy baths she loved.

The bedroom was larger than she expected. One window looked out on a disreputable alley, but the other offered a view of the neighbor's garden, which she was sure would be lovely in the spring. She thought of her own pretty patch of flowers behind the townhouse. She'd neglected her garden the past couple of years, but she would miss it when spring came.

"So what do you think, Mrs. Jernigan?" the little man asked eagerly.

She hesitated, then smiled and nodded. So it needed a little paint, some minor repairs. It was a palace compared to some of the other places she'd seen. She could whip it into shape. With some pretty curtains, a throw rug here and there... yes, this would do.

She wrote out a check for the deposit, again wiping out her bank account. The man handed her the rental application, which she filled out on the spot and returned to him.

He perused it briefly, nodding in satisfaction. "I'll call as soon as you're approved. Just a formality, of course, in your case, you being president of a big company and all." He glanced meaningfully at the fur draped over her arm.

Halley thanked him and left. She considered the subway, but it was getting dark. Instead she walked to the nearest busy intersection and waved down a cab. She couldn't really afford it, but neither could she afford to get herself mugged.

Jay was already home by the time she arrived. "Where have you been?" he demanded the moment she walked through the door.

She stared at him, surprised. "I've been looking at apartments. Why, is something wrong?"

Jay sighed and rubbed the back of his head, relaxing visibly. "No. Sorry, I didn't mean to bark, but I was worried. I called your office to tell you I was bringing home a pizza, and Kathryn said you'd gone home shortly after lunch, that you had a headache or something. Why didn't you just tell her the truth?"

Halley set her purse down and unbuttoned her coat, irrationally warmed by Jay's concern. "Kathryn doesn't know about the divorce. No one knows."

"Why not?"

"Because I don't want everyone tiptoeing around me, pitying me or trying to get me to 'share my feelings.' I'm just not ready for people to know."

Jay nodded. "Right. People can be such a pain in the ass when they care about you."

She looked up sharply at his acid tone, but before she could comment on his unappreciated sarcasm, he'd spoken again.

"Pizza's in the oven and beer's in the fridge whenever you want it."

The idea of food didn't appeal to her. She moved toward the beckoning warmth of the stove and held her hands out toward it.

"So, how's the apartment search going?" Jay asked.

"Eager to be rid of me?" She offered a tentative smile.

"No, I already told you you're welcome to stay till you find a place." He gave a long-suffering sigh. "I'm just politely interested, that's all."

"I did find a place, as a matter of fact."

He raised one curious eyebrow, but gave no further hint of his feelings about her news.

"It's in Chelsea, and not a bad neighborhood at all," she elaborated, forcing a bit more enthusiasm than she actually had. "The building has old world charm—you know, lots of wood, high ceilings . . ."

"Is it safe?" Jay asked immediately.

"Oh, yes, I'd say so. The manager has promised a new lock, a good strong dead bolt. It's nice and airy..." She looked around her, seeing their comfortably furnished townhouse with a fresh eye, its gleaming wood floors and pastel walls suddenly dear to her. All at once, images bombarded her: newspaper on the front lawn, peeling paint, stale cooking odors no disinfectant could mask, a dingy, mildewed bathroom, and the tiniest movement in the kitchen she'd seen from the corner of her eye, but which she'd forced herself to ignore at the time—

"Halley?"

All at once tears welled up in her eyes and overflowed in a flash flood. They were coursing down her cheeks before she could stop them or hide them, before she could escape. She couldn't seem to move, wrapped in a smothering, blinding cocoon of hopelessness. So she stood there and sobbed like a ninny in front of Jay, which only made everything worse.

He thrust a paper napkin into her hand. She mopped up some of the tears and blew her nose, but the horrible sobs just kept coming and coming.

She felt a strong arm slide around her shoulders. She tried to shake it off, but it was persistent, pulling her toward a great expanse of sweater. She struggled in earnest and found herself unceremoniously hauled against a hard, warm chest.

"Dammit, Halley, would you relax and let yourself cry?"

"No! Let go of me."

"I will not. For God's sake, woman, you can't keep everything bottled up inside of you, or one of these days you're going to explode." Despite her protests, he scooped her up and carried her to the sofa.

"Let me go, you big Swedish meatball," she choked out between sobs, striking ineffectually at his chest.

"Will you stop fighting me? Just what the hell are you so afraid of? If you're worried that I might jump you, you can forget that. Right now you're about as appealing as a turnip. Now stop acting like a martyr and cry on my shoulder. I'm not letting you go until you do."

She stopped struggling, knowing it was futile, and slumped against Jay's shoulder, defeated. "Do you have any idea how ridiculous you sound, demanding that I cry on you?" She almost giggled, then, but it turned into another wracking sob. Her eyes overflowed again, in impossible torrents, until she'd soaked the front of his sweater. She didn't even try to stop; she just kept crying until she couldn't force one more tear.

The moment she'd given in, all the anger left Jay. He held her against him, stroking her hair, murmuring soft, meaningless words of comfort. He hadn't meant to bully her, but he was convinced she needed this.

Perhaps he needed it even more.

He continued to hold her close, with her head nestled in the hollow of his shoulder. Though she'd stopped crying, he was loath to let her go. She felt good in his arms—warm, soft, and tempting. A bit too tempting, he decided, laying his cheek against her softly scented hair.

"Feel better now?" he asked her.

"No. I feel silly and embarrassed and pitiful, not to mention totally unappealing. You called me a turnip," she accused, though she didn't put much bite into the charge.

"I meant a pretty turnip," he clarified with a twinge of guilt. Maybe he shouldn't have been so hard on her.

"Put a sock in it, Jay." She pulled away from him.

Reluctantly he released her. He'd accomplished what he wanted, after all. She'd allowed him to comfort her, never mind how grudgingly, and never mind how grumpy she was now. "Would you have preferred to be compared to a rutabaga?" he asked with genuine-sounding concern.

As she stood she gave him a look, *the* look, the one she reserved for when he was treading dangerous territory. But he thought he detected a tremor of mirth lurking at the corners of her mouth.

"If you're done comparing me to tuberous roots, I'm going to soak in a hot bath," she declared, stretching elaborately. Her movements caused the hem of her sweater to creep above the waistband of her shirt, revealing the pale silk of a teddy.

Jay caught himself just short of reaching up to touch the smooth, gossamer fabric. He was a sucker for sexy underwear, especially when she wore it under her business clothes, and he was the only one who knew it was there. There had been days—they seemed a long time ago—when he'd spent hours on end thinking of nothing but coming home at five o'clock and peeling Halley's clothes off layer by layer to reveal the sexily wrapped package underneath all the crepe and wool.

"While I'm gone I'll expect you to forget this crying business," she continued in a stern voice, obviously unaware of the inappropriate direction of his thoughts. She started to leave, then paused, adding, "Save some pizza for me," before disappearing.

Jay took several deep, cleansing breaths and scanned the room for something neutral on which to focus his gaze—anything to banish the fantasy images that threatened, mental pictures of Halley undressing for her bath, revealing the creamy undergarment he'd just glimpsed. He forced himself to stare at the toes of his socks, the most unromantic subject he could find. They didn't match, he noticed, but he wasn't surprised. When he did his own laundry, socks had a way of disappearing, until finding two that matched became a task too daunting for his sleep-blurry mornings.

With such mundane thoughts, he was successful in chasing away all forbidden imaginings of Halley. Gradually he relaxed and allowed himself a smile, pleased with his control.

In fact, he was pleased altogether. Whether she admitted it or not, the crying jag had done Halley some good. At least she was calm, now, not overly bright and breathless as she'd been a few minutes ago. She seemed to have uncoiled a little, like an overwound watch spring that had ticked itself frantically back to normal.

As soon as he heard the water draining in the bathroom, he removed the pizza box from the oven and set it on the coffee table. He set out plates, forks, and napkins, then two cold beers. He opened the armoire that housed his television and turned on an old movie, so they wouldn't have to talk if Halley didn't want to.

She emerged from the bathroom a couple of minutes later, wrapped in a plush terry robe. Her hair was pinned carelessly atop her head and her skin looked fresh and pink, free of makeup. Though he appreciated her glamorous side, Jay found her disturbingly alluring like this—imminently touchable, and nothing at all like a turnip.

"What's the movie?" she asked, settling on the floor a safe distance away from him.

"Dunno. I just turned it on. But Cary Grant is in it."

"Good. I hope it's a mindless comedy. That's just what I need." She served herself some pizza with slow, easy movements, looking more relaxed than she'd been since returning from Europe. Again he congratulated himself for handling the situation correctly.

"Did I get any mail today?" she asked, her eyes focused on the TV screen.

"Uh, yeah, it's around here somewhere," he answered vaguely. Her Visa bill had arrived, and he didn't want to ruin her dinner.

For a while the room was quiet, with just the sound of the TV and an occasional chuckle to punctuate the silence.

Though Jay had told himself he'd do nothing to aggravate Halley's distress or remind her of her problems, he had to speak his mind about this apartment she planned to rent.

"So is the apartment really bad?" he asked casually when a commercial came on.

She picked up the remote control and muted the TV, then turned her full attention on him. "It's not the Taj Mahal, but it's not the Black Hole of Calcutta, either. I'll survive it. It's only for a few months, till I get on my feet again."

Jay shuddered to think of Halley living in some rat's nest. "For what it's worth," he said cautiously, "I don't think you should take it. I'm sure something better will come along."

"If it did, I wouldn't be able to afford it. No, I think this is about the best I can do. Besides, I already put a deposit down on it. As soon as the manager okays my credit, I can move in." She took another bite of pizza. "Where did you say the mail was?"

"I didn't. Maybe it's in the kitchen," he mumbled. But his disinterest didn't catch on.

Halley pushed herself up off the floor and went to look for the mail. "I'm expecting an invitation to a baby shower—one of my former models. That's one career shot to hell." She made a cursory search of the living room, then the kitchen. "I won't be able to go, but I ought to send a gift."

She at last found the mail on the table in the entry hall, where Jay had known it was all along, and returned triumphant to finish her pizza and sort through the letters.

Though Jay pretended interest in the movie, he could tell when she found the bill. He heard the soft intake of breath, the quiet sigh, then the frantic ripping of the envelope and unfolding of paper. Then, finally, a hopeless-sounding groan.

"How could one person possibly spend this much money?" she asked rhetorically.

"Hmm?" Jay said, as if he hadn't been paying attention.

"My Visa statement. It looks like I singlehandedly boosted the economies of several European countries over the past few weeks." She no longer appeared relaxed.

Silently Jay cursed the Postal Service for its lousy timing. It could have delayed delivery of the bill another day or two.

With a dismissive gesture, she refolded the invoice and tucked it into the envelope. "Oh, well. They'll just have to take a number." She pushed the mail aside, seemingly no longer interested, and riveted her gaze on the TV screen. She nursed a beer right out of the can, ignoring the frosted mug Jay had provided, and said nothing else for the duration of the movie. She didn't laugh at all.

They said their awkward good-nights as soon as the film was over, retreating to their separate rooms. Jay lay awake a long time, wondering how he could help Halley. He knew damn well it wasn't his place to interfere, and she wouldn't allow his help anyway. That infuriating pride of hers would be her downfall, he thought, belligerently punching his pillow. He ought to just let her wallow in it and see how much comfort it gets her.

But he couldn't. He had to at least try to give her a hand, even if he was forced to do it clandestinely. He simply couldn't allow her to ruin her credit because of some unforeseen calamity. And he absolutely couldn't stand idly by and watch her move into some hovel where she wasn't even safe, let alone comfortable.

By the time he finally fell asleep, he'd settled on a plan.

He made it a point to get up before Halley the next morning. Showered, shaved, and dressed in record time, he wandered through the living room toward the kitchen, casually picking up Halley's Visa bill on the way and tucking it into his back pocket.

He started the coffee, then went to the entry hall and the coat tree, where Halley had hung her fur and her suede handbag. This was the part he wasn't sure he could go through with—actually opening the purse and invading her privacy. He reached for the bag twice, stopping himself each time. Maybe this was too sneaky.

Just as he was about to give up the idea, he saw the corner of a newspaper—the classifieds—sticking out of her coat pocket. He could see part of one ad, circled in red, without even touching the coat. Satisfied that this was an acceptable level of snooping, he bent closer to read what he could, then almost wished he hadn't. Was this the apartment she'd rented? In the Aurora Gardens district of Chelsea? That was an *awful* area.

He memorized the phone number.

He had time for a quick cup of coffee before Halley appeared, wearing a teal blue sweater dress cinched tightly around her narrow waist. She'd woven a grosgrain ribbon into her braid, and not a hair was out of place. She was once again her cool, professional self. Jay couldn't help but admire her ability to appear so in control when he knew she was brimming with anxiety.

But he didn't like seeing her so serious this early in the morning. He wished he had time to cajole her out of that businesslike demeanor, the way he used to. On a good morning, when he was feeling particularly mischievous, he might have even cajoled her right out of her clothes. That was obviously not an option today.

"Coffee's ready," he offered, shrugging into his down jacket. A hasty departure was in his best interest, before he gave away something he shouldn't. "I have to go."

She awarded him a wildly curious look. "I thought you made it a rule to avoid early morning appointments."

"Sometimes certain responsibilities are unavoidable," he explained on his way out the door. He wasn't a very accomplished liar. Halley could always tell when something was up with him, and he didn't want to give her the opportunity to question him further.

The studio was dark and cold when he arrived. He flipped on lights haphazardly as he made his way to the office he and Peg shared, pausing at the doorway to bump the thermostat up a few notches. Then he went straight to the phone without bothering to take his coat off. He removed one glove and dialed the number he'd memorized.

"I'm calling about the apartment," he said when a man answered.

"Sorry, it's been rented."

"I know," Jay said hastily, before the man could hang up. "To a Halley Jernigan?"

Silence. Then, reluctantly, "Maybe. Who's asking?"

Jay hadn't considered exactly how he would word his request. He decided the truth was probably his best bet. "This is her ex-husband."

"Me and my big mouth," the man said disgustedly. "If you're her ex, what business is it of yours where she lives? 'Cause if you got in mind to harass her or something—"

"No, it's not like that. I just want her to find a nicer place to live, that's all."

"What do you mean, *nicer?*" the man bellowed. "I keep a clean building here. No hookers, no pushers—"

"I didn't mean it like that," Jay interjected quickly, trying to repair the damage. "What I mean is, Halley is a very classy lady, and she belongs somewhere more..." He stopped just short of verbalizing another insult.

"Look, whaddya want me to do," the other man said. "She put down a deposit, and if her credit checks out she gets the apartment."

"I'll pay you twice the deposit if you'll turn her down."

"*What?* You nuts or something?"

"I'll send the payment by messenger today. Just tell her you can't rent to her, because her finances aren't up to par. You won't be lying," he added. "She is having financial problems."

More silence. Then, "You'd pay me twice the deposit just to rent the apartment to someone else, right?"

"Yup."

His hesitation did an abrupt disappearing act. "Make the check out to Fred M. Campbell. That's *M* as in Mother."

They settled on an amount. Jay wrote out the check and called a messenger service. And as long as he had the checkbook out...he extracted Halley's bill from his pocket and considered the multidigit balance. Business at his studio had been exceptionally good the last few weeks, so he could afford to indulge an impulse. He made the check out for the whole thing.

Four

―――

"Hello there," Kathryn sang out cheerily as Halley whisked into the office later that morning, still shaking off the cold. She had just come from a disappointing meeting with a bank vice president, who had told her in no uncertain terms that her credit could be extended no further.

"You've got a bizillion messages," Kathryn continued. "TNT definitely wants four of our models for the video."

"Ah, no wonder you're so perky," Halley said, her flagging enthusiasm for the morning reviving a bit at the good news. Maybe she could pay herself this week after all.

"We also got a check from *Pizzazz* magazine in the mail." Kathryn paused to take a phone call, giving the automatic answers Halley had heard a million times: "Five foot eight, one hundred fifteen pounds is our current standard . . . No, I wouldn't advise flying to New York just yet. Send us five or six pictures. We'll call if we're interested."

Every time she heard this speech, Halley felt a pang of compassion for the fresh-faced young woman who was undoubtedly on the receiving end. There were so many girls out there—prom queens and county fair pageant winners from all over the country, desperately wanting to model in New York. She herself had been lucky, damned lucky, that an agent had picked her out of a crowd of photos and invited her for an interview, eventually paving the way for her escape from an intolerable situation at home. She tried to remember that every time she rejected a hopeful applicant.

"Any thing else important?" she asked when Kathryn finished with the caller.

"Just something curious." She rifled through a stack of pink message slips. "Here it is. A Mr. Campbell called from the Cheshire Arms apartments," she read. "He said he's refusing your application. I told him I thought he had the wrong person, but—"

Halley groaned. "This is unbelievable. Are you sure that's what he said?"

Kathryn looked insulted. "I'm sure. He said your finances weren't up to snuff—his words exactly—and he'd tear up your deposit check."

Halley let loose a colorful curse.

Kathryn blanched. "What's the deal, Halley? You and Jay aren't moving out of that darling townhouse, are you?"

Several evasive answers came to Halley's mind, but she dismissed them all. It was time for her to come clean. Kathryn had been a loyal friend for years; it wasn't right to keep a secret like this from her. "Jay and I have split up," she said, keeping her voice carefully neutral. "The divorce was final about a week ago."

Kathryn's mouth hung open in shock. "Why didn't you say something?" she managed to choke out.

"I should have," Halley answered simply, unable to adequately explain her reluctance to confide in Kathryn, as compassionate and discreet a friend as anyone could want.

"Where are you living now?"

"Still with Jay," she admitted with a rueful grin. "He's been unbelievably noble about the difficulty I've had getting moved out. This financial crisis has ruined my plans. I thought I had a new place to live all sewed up, but apparently I don't even qualify to move into a dump like the Cheshire Arms."

"But what happened?" Kathryn asked, sounding completely devastated. "The two of you were so...happy, I thought."

"We were, once." Halley's vision blurred as she remembered the joyous, breathlessly loving couple they'd once been. "I don't know what happened. We grew in different directions, I guess. Things got complicated...we just weren't on the same wavelength. That sounds incredibly cliché, doesn't it?"

Kathryn didn't answer. Her eyes were unusually shiny, and her lips were pressed together in a tight line as she looked anywhere but at her employer.

"Don't cry, and that's an order," Halley said. "I'm okay, Jay's okay. It's been a very civil divorce. In fact, now that the marriage is over, we're getting along better than we have in months." She had to wonder why that was true. Perhaps it was just a case of the pressure finally being off.

"You mean you haven't painted a dividing line down the middle of your house?" Kathryn asked, trying hard to make light of the situation.

Halley chuckled, appreciating her receptionist's savvy. Kathryn knew she wouldn't want pity or maudlin sentiments. "Not so far. But we may come to that if I don't find a place to live soon."

"You could move in with me," Kathryn offered immediately, as Halley had known she would. "We have a fold-
out bed in the living room, and I know my roommates
wouldn't mind—oh, but wait, I forgot. Sherry's cousin is
staying with us for a couple of weeks. But if you wanted to
borrow my sleeping bag . . . No, I guess not," she said before Halley could accept or decline. "You'd have to wait in
line for the bathroom every morning, and I don't know
where you would put your clothes. You'd hate it."

In a way Halley was glad Kathryn had withdrawn her im-
pulsive offer. Though Halley would have jumped at any
reasonable alternative to remaining under Jay's roof, five
women sharing two rooms and one bath simply wasn't
workable.

"Thanks just the same, Kath," she said, "but I'll stick it
out with Jay awhile longer. Surely my luck has to change
soon."

Kathryn schooled her face and returned to other pressing
matters. "Don't forget, you have lunch with *her* today. She
called to confirm, 'just to make sure this time, darling.'"

Halley had to grin at Kathryn's flawless imitation of
Maureen. But the grin faded almost immediately. The model
had been calling every day, asking for Harold. As much as
Halley disliked the notion, she'd have to tell Maureen about
Harold's perfidy, then swear her to secrecy and hope for the
best. Lunch was the best opportunity she'd get.

"I've made reservations at Don Juan's," Maureen said as
she and Halley stepped outside into the wetly falling snow
at half past twelve. "Here, sweetie, get under my umbrella
before you get that delicious fox all wet. You know, I'd kill
to get that fur. I've never seen anything like it."

Halley hugged the coat closer to her, to ward off the chill.
She had ordered the fox specially made for her last year as
a reward for some major milestone in her business. Wear-

ing it made her feel like a success. Perhaps that's why she wore it constantly these days. It reminded her of success, of wealth, and of all the things she stood to regain if she could just hold on these next few weeks.

"Um, Maureen, would you mind awfully if we skipped Don Juan's and picked up a couple of sandwiches at the Sub Stop instead?"

Maureen halted abruptly, causing Halley to bump her forehead on the edge of the umbrella. "What, are you joking?"

"I can't afford Don Juan's. I have nine dollars on me, and that includes my subway fare home. So let's just get some sandwiches, and I'll tell you the whole ugly story."

Maureen's face lit up at the prospect. "I can't wait. But a tale of such obvious woe deserves better than some dry sandwich. It has to be Don Juan's, and you'll be my guest, of course. Keep the nine dollars and at least take a taxi, for goodness sake. The subway is so bourgeois."

Halley accepted Maureen's offer, charity or no. At least Don Juan's heavenly spinach soufflé would soften the task ahead of her.

In their corner booth, Maureen's eyes grew larger and larger and her jaw dropped lower and lower as the unsavory tale unfolded. "Oh, sweetie, I had no idea. That rotten little Harold! And to think I let him—never mind. Why, Halley, this could ruin you! How are you going to keep this a secret? If any of your clients find out—"

"Of course I can count on your discretion," Halley cut in, giving Maureen an even stare.

"Oh, of *course*. So you think you'll be able to weather the storm, then?" Maureen asked anxiously.

"Barring any further disasters...yes, I plan to survive and come out of this just fine." She found that saying the words aloud gave the prediction a sense of reality.

"But some extra cash flow wouldn't hurt, I bet," Maureen said, her eyes narrowed calculatingly. "Do you know how much money I can make in a week?"

Halley sighed impatiently. "We've been over this before. I wish I could represent you, but your...style just isn't compatible with the Mystique Agency." That was as kindly as she could put it.

"I'm too old, is that it? Because you know, I was talking to this plastic surgeon—"

"No, Maureen, it has nothing to do with your age. I represent at least three models who are older than you. It's your...image. It's a fine image for you," Halley rushed on, "but it just doesn't—"

"Oh, never mind," Maureen cut in sharply. "You know, for someone crying poor, you make some awfully dumb decisions. Like that coat." She nodded toward the blue fox lying on the chair next to Halley. "You should sell it. Why, I'd give you five thousand for it in the blink of an eye. Cash."

Halley held her breath and silently counted to ten, then twenty. Sell her coat? She'd sooner cut off her right arm. "No, thanks, Maureen," she said sweetly.

Halley made beef stew for dinner that night, along with a big salad and some biscuits baked from scratch. Not gourmet fare, but it filled the apartment with a warm, inviting fragrance. She found that the cooking tasks—chopping, measuring, stirring—served to calm her down, to de-stress her. Though Maureen's condescending offer had put a damper on the whole afternoon, Halley was actually humming by the time Jay got home around seven.

"You look awfully domestic," he said with a wink, taking an unsolicited taste test from the stew pot. "Mmm, just like your mother's."

"It should be. It's her recipe."

"You really don't have to do this, you know," he said cautiously. "You did the modeling for me. We're even."

"Not for long. My apartment fell through. I'm back to square one, so you're stuck with me awhile longer. Anyway, I'm enjoying myself," she said, placing the last round biscuit into a pan with the others. "I'd forgotten how much fun it is to cook. Certainly takes my mind off my problems."

"Are they so bad? Your problems, that is?"

She shrugged as she put the biscuits in the oven, then winced and rubbed the back of her neck. "I've kept the wolf at bay another day. It's not that bad. But I've got a whole slew of these tension knots—" She halted self-consciously.

Jay had already suspected she had muscle spasms. He could tell by the way she held her neck and shoulders. He also knew why she'd cut her sentence short. In the past, whenever an attack of stress had settled in her neck, he'd treat her to his own version of a Swedish massage. The full treatment involved warm lotion and a distinct lack of clothing.

"I'll set the table," he said a bit gruffly, grabbing plates and bowls from the cabinet. Why did she have to say anything about tension knots? Now he'd never get his mind off it, off her, how her satin skin felt under his lotion-slick hands, and how, when he'd worked every knot out, he'd continued to massage every inch of her body, watching her go from tense to relaxed to aroused... "Dammit!"

"Something wrong?" she called from the kitchen.

"Nothing I, um, dropped a fork," he called from the dining room. *But dammit anyway,* he added silently. He'd had no idea the difficulties involved with allowing Halley to stay here. Not that he'd do it any differently if he had the decision to make again. He couldn't put her out on the street. But living with her in such close confines, seeing her every day, smelling her perfume at every turn, sitting across from her at the table most every night—it was enough to drive a man insane. Things had never been this strained between them, not even during the tense months before the divorce, he thought as he set butter, salt, and pepper on the table. Back then they'd avoided each other by working long hours or staying out late with friends. Jay had spent more nights sprawled out on a cot in his darkroom than he'd care to remember, just so he wouldn't have to face her, knowing she would be leaving him.

He had no desire to avoid her now. Even though they were awkward around one another, he made it a point to be home for dinner. Even though he took frequent, long walks in the cold, he craved her company. Just looking at her, hearing her voice, gave him pleasure mixed with a dose of poignant pain, yet he couldn't cut himself off from her.

Something had changed. The bitterness, once so much a part of them, had evaporated. Was that what divorce did? Had the signing of that legal document dissolving their marriage also taken away their reasons for clashing? Somehow he didn't think that was it. He knew enough divorced couples who still fought like sewer rats.

"It's ready," Halley announced as she carried a silver soup tureen into the dining room.

Jay smiled at the incongruity of beef stew in such a fancy receptacle. Still, that was something Halley would do. The tureen was a wedding gift, he remembered, though he couldn't recall who from. He ought to give it to her, he decided. It was a little too feminine looking for a man living alone.

Halley made a second trip from the kitchen with the golden biscuits and a pitcher of ice water. Jay realized he ought to be helping, but everything seemed to be done. Instead he pulled her chair out for her, and immediately decided it was too polite a gesture, like something a man does when he's trying to impress a woman.

She didn't seem to mind.

"The stew is wonderful," he commented as he ladled a second helping into his bowl a few minutes later. "When did you learn to cook like this?"

"I've always known how. My mother forced me to learn. She insisted it was one of those things that a woman *had* to know if she wanted to catch—or keep—her man." Halley laughed, though without humor. "As if Dad would have left if she hadn't been able to broil a decent pork chop." She paused, looking pensive. "Still, sometimes I wonder if I shouldn't have ... well, been a little more domestic. I don't mean give up my career, but lots of women have demanding careers and still manage to cook and clean—"

"Don't, Halley."

"Don't what?"

"Don't play 'what if' with our marriage. We both made choices, did things we had to, because of who we are. I didn't marry you for your cooking abilities, and we didn't split up because you *didn't* cook, either. You'll drive yourself crazy if you start thinking that way."

"Why *did* you marry me?" she asked abruptly.

He stared at her, hard. "It's a little late for that question, don't you think?"

"It just suddenly occurred to me that I still don't know what brought us together in the first place. I know we were relatively young when we got married, but are we really so different now than we were then?"

"In some respects, yeah," Jay said. "We were both just starting out, ambitious, hungry. We had a lot in common. And now, well ..."

"Ambition and hunger? Surely there was more to it than that."

A physical attraction that bordered on obsession, Jay thought. "Do we have to talk about this? I'll be the first to admit that we should have done more talking before the divorce, but it's too late now. I'm not fond of postmortems."

"Oh." She stared into her empty bowl, unconsciously hunching her shoulders, then rubbing the back of her neck. "I'm sorry if I made you uncomfortable."

"Speaking of discomfort, you ought to do something about your neck. You look miserable."

"I'll take a hot bath," she said dismissively.

Jay was already rising out of his chair. "That doesn't do the trick. Will you let me help?"

She jerked her head up and stared at him, her initial reaction one of alarm.

He stopped halfway around the table, still several feet away from her, holding his palms up in a gesture of innocence. "No ulterior motives, okay? We'll do it right here at the dinner table, fully clothed. The moment you feel uncomfortable, I'll stop."

Halley had to laugh. For one panicky instant, a great seduction scene had flashed before her eyes. But that's obviously not what Jay had in mind. "Okay, okay," she said. "You're the only person I know who can work these knots out."

He was already standing behind her. "Let's start by undoing this tight braid," he said, pulling out the elastic band and unraveling her dark mahogany hair.

She knew she'd made a mistake. She should have simply put up with the tension in her neck. But now here he was, his hands tangled in her hair, his fingers massaging her scalp. She might still have objected, if it hadn't felt so damn good.

His fingers, strong and sure, worked their way across her forehead, down her temples, and finally to a point behind her ears. "Breath slowly," he said. "In . . . and out."

She tried, not very successfully.

He pressed his thumbs against the base of her skull, then the back of her neck, gradually working his way down, vertebra by vertebra, as his fingertips brushed lightly against her skin.

"I've always wondered where you learned to do this," she said, half-swooning at the acute pleasure his talented fingers could bring her. And he was only touching her neck.

"I'm Swedish," he replied. "It's in my genes. Lean forward."

She did, resting her forearms on the table, then cradling her head against them. His hands began a slow massage of her shoulders, his sensitive fingers locating each knot and working it until it dissolved. Without meaning to, Halley moaned.

"Does that hurt?" he asked, lightening his touch.

"Feels good," she mumbled, past caring where or how he touched her. "Don't stop." All she knew was that she felt delicious, all the way down to her toes. She found that she could forget everything except the feel of his warm touch, and forgetting was something she needed right now.

Jay wasn't forgetting, but remembering. He remembered all too clearly the silken texture of her skin as he relived it. He remembered what it felt like to run his hands down Halley's lean, trim back, to feel her flesh quiver in response to his touch. Slowly he unzipped the back of her dress, already knowing she would not object. She was in that relaxed state, somewhere between waking and sleeping, when she was highly suggestible. He knew it was wrong to take advantage of her momentary complacence, but he couldn't seem to stop touching her. To pull away now would require more strength than he could muster.

Would she be so accepting of his attentions if she knew he'd sabotaged her apartment deal? he wondered. The flash of guilt shot painfully through him.

He slid his hands beneath the dress, massaging her shoulder blades, pressing his fingers around their pleasing contours, remembering. And knowing he had to stop. He pressed his hands full against her, closing his eyes, as if memorizing again the feel of her. Then he took a deep breath, withdrew, and zipped up her dress.

"Halley?"

"Mmmmm?"

"I'm done." But he left his hands resting easily on her shoulders.

"Mmmmm." She didn't lift her head.

"Now that you're all nice and relaxed, I have something to tell you." He had to get his duplicity out in the open.

"What is it?" she said through a yawn, slowly lifting her head.

"I know why you didn't get that apartment you wanted."

"Lousy credit?"

"No. I paid off the manager to turn you down."

"You *what?*"

He felt her immediately tense beneath his hands. Without even thinking about it, he resumed a slow massage. "I didn't want you living in that disgusting place. It's not safe." Though he couldn't see her face, he could see the color rising in her neck.

"Since when was that your decision to make?" she asked in a deceptively calm voice.

"It wasn't," he acknowledged. "But I did it anyway, and I'm not sorry. You don't belong in a place like that."

"But I don't belong here, either!" she said, suddenly intense and fully awake once more. She brushed his hands off her shoulders and stood to face him. "What is it, you *want* me dependent on you? Does that make you feel macho?" She saw the look of pain her harsh words inflicted and knew regret. "I didn't mean that. I know you think you're helping, but you don't have to help me anymore. I'm on my own, now, and I'll solve my own problems."

Jay let out a harsh sound—it could have been a laugh, or a hopeless sigh. "You've always been on your own, Halley.

Through six years of marriage, you were always on your own. One of these days you're going to need someone—"

"I do need you, Jay," she said softly. "I couldn't have gotten by without your help."

"You needed a roof over your head and a few groceries. Anyone could have helped you. I'm not talking about that kind of need. I'm talking about when you need someone here." He started to touch his finger to the space over her heart, then changed his mind and touched his own breastbone instead. "When you need someone to accept you without question. When you need someone to be there—to just be there for you. When that time comes, I sure as hell hope it's not me you need, 'cause I might not be around." He whirled and stalked away, slamming the bedroom door.

She stared after him, bewildered. What the heck was he talking about? He'd done her out of an apartment, she'd gotten justifiably angry about it, and suddenly she was an ogre. What had she missed?

The door opened again. "Oh, by the way, as long as you're already mad at me, I might as well confess everything. I paid off your Visa balance." The door closed again before Halley could do anything but give a little gasp of surprise.

She started for the door, stopped, tried to think. The last thing she needed to do was barge into the bedroom—*Jay's* bedroom—and completely lose her cool. Instead she turned very slowly and began clearing the table.

Her hands trembled, she was so furious, yet not quite furious enough to give Jay the piece of her mind he deserved. How dare he interfere so blatantly with her life. Now she was in debt to him for . . . Good Lord, her balance had been over three thousand dollars. She'd much rather owe her bank than her ex-husband. A credit card debt was simple—she would pay the bill and the bank would be satisfied. But now she owed Jay her gratitude in addition to money. Even after she paid him back, he could always hold it over her head that he'd bailed her out.

Let's be fair, she scolded herself as she loaded the dishwasher. When had Jay ever held anything over her head? Then again, when had she ever been in debt to him?

He was only trying to help, she reasoned. But that explanation simply didn't cover all the bases. It all went back to what he'd said about her needing someone. He wanted her to need him. She didn't want to need *anyone*. Need led to dependence, and dependence led to weakness. She'd seen it herself, watched it every day while she was growing up. And she'd be damned if she'd put herself in the same position her mother had.

She sighed as she closed the dishwasher and turned it on. Her situation with Jay wasn't the same as that of her parents, not at all. Jay had never expected dinner on the table by six or clean socks every morning. He'd never tried to prevent her from following her dream. She was more mature and more in control of her life than her mother had ever been.

So he'd paid off her credit card, she thought, feeling herself growing calmer. She could live with that. She would simply pay him back at the first opportunity.

When she opened the refrigerator to put away the leftover stew, she discovered the cheesecake she'd made earlier. It was the instant kind, nothing fancy, but Jay had always loved it. She couldn't believe she'd forgotten about dessert.

Maybe it wasn't too late. Impulsively she took the cake out of the fridge and cut a generous slice. Moments later she was standing outside the bedroom door, knocking tentatively. She'd decided that if Jay didn't answer, she'd retreat and eat the dessert herself.

"Come in," he called, sounding just as uncertain as she felt.

She entered briskly, holding the plate out as a peace offering. "I forgot we had dessert," she said, looking first at him and then up at the ceiling. She hadn't realized until she was already in the room that he was stretched out on the bed in nothing but those damned white gym shorts.

He sat up quickly, grabbing his discarded sweatshirt. "It's cheesecake," he said, a trace of wonder in his voice.

"It's just the kind out of a box." She chanced a look at him now that he was more or less covered. He appeared a bit confused as he took the plate and fork, as if he expected her to bolt the moment she'd handed it over. Instead she sat down on the corner of the bed, a nice, safe distance from him.

"It's good," he said, savoring a small bite. "Aren't you having some?"

She shook her head. "I'm sorry I blew up at you," she said suddenly.

To her surprise he smiled. "Why? I deserved it. I even expected it. I was meddling."

"If you knew that, then why did you do it?" she asked, not condemning but merely curious. She wanted to comprehend his reasoning.

"I was compelled. I literally could not stop myself. I don't expect you to understand that."

"But if you knew I would get mad, then why did you get mad back?"

He shrugged. "You pushed the wrong button, that's all. Do you want a bite of cheesecake?"

"No, thanks. Jay?"

He raised his eyebrows questioningly.

She struggled with the next few words. "Thank you for saving me from the Cheshire Arms. That apartment had mice."

"Thank you?" he repeated.

"And th-thank you for paying off my credit card."

He grinned, as if he'd just understood some private joke. "I expect to be paid back," he said.

"Every cent," she agreed. "Weekly installments starting...next week?"

He nodded.

That wasn't so difficult, she noted. Maybe she had wasted a good temper tantrum over this. Then again, she *was* letting Jay off the hook—something she never would have done if they were still married. "Jay, just one more thing. Don't do this again, okay?"

He had the good grace to look sheepish. "I'll make a deal with you. I won't do any more meddling if you'll do something for me."

"What?" She shivered inside, half-terrified of what he might want.

"Ask. If you get into a bind, please ask me for help. If I can, I will, no strings attached. I'll sleep better knowing you're not heading for bankruptcy."

She nodded with a small, relieved smile. "Deal. I won't let them drag me off to debtors' prison without sending out a distress signal first."

They sat staring foolishly at each other for several silent seconds. Jay felt irrationally happy that his subterfuge was out in the open. The storm of her anger had passed much more quickly than he had expected, leaving only a few errant flashes of lightning that spoke of something besides anger.

In the space of a few heartbeats the mood between them changed subtly to one of possibilities. Halley looked beautiful to him, with her hair in uncharacteristic disarray and that sweater dress clinging to every feminine curve. He thought he knew every inch of her, from both a photographer's and a lover's point of view, but suddenly he saw her with fresh eyes.

They stared only a few more seconds before Halley broke eye contact. She stood too quickly and reached for the empty plate and fork, which Jay had laid down on the night stand. "I'll just take this to the kitchen," she said, trying to assume a businesslike tone, though her breathlessness gave her away.

Jay started to halt her, to tell her he could take care of his own dishes, that she didn't have to wait on him. But if he opened his mouth at all, he was afraid he'd say something else, something to the effect of "Don't go, stay with me." So he clamped his mouth shut.

When he was alone again, he acknowledged that he was indeed a true gentleman. Only a gentleman would have let her walk out of his bedroom, looking like that, without a struggle.

Five

Halley had just sat down at her desk to go over the accounts when the phone buzzed. She punched the white intercom button. "What is it, Kathryn?" she asked wearily.

"Jay is here," Kathryn announced, unable to mask her surprise. "Should I send him back?"

Halley sat up straighter. Lordy, she was a mess, and she hated to receive surprise visitors. Nonetheless, she could hardly refuse to see Jay. He wouldn't be here without a good reason, she surmised. "Give me three minutes, then send him back," she answered, pushing her tired feet back into her punishing pumps.

Three minutes to pull herself together. Halley pushed herself away from her desk and whisked into the private powder room adjacent to her office. The mirror confirmed her worst expectations. "Unmade bed," she said aloud, coldly assessing the shadows under her eyes and the chapped lips. Two dots of highlighter and a fresh coat of lipstick helped some, although she belatedly wished she'd chosen a less severe color. Or maybe it was her hair that was too severe, she decided, pulling a few tendrils loose from the tight chignon.

She heard her office door open and Jay's muffled voice. "Halley?"

"I'll be out in a minute," she called as her heart pounded and her palms became damp. What was wrong with her? She was reacting as though she were meeting a man for their first date, not her ex-husband.

It was just the surprise of him visiting here, she told herself. In the two years since she'd moved to the Korman Building, Jay had been here exactly once—for her gala opening—and even then she'd had to practically drag him.

Quickly she grabbed a bottle of cologne and spritzed herself, realizing too late that she'd just used Jay's favorite scent. Great, no telling what he would think.

She emerged from the powder room with a confident, if counterfeit, smile firmly in place. "Fancy seeing you here," she said, as surprised by what he wore as she was by his presence in general. He was dressed in crisply pressed trousers, starched white shirt, tweed jacket, and silk tie—the last, a gift from her. She hadn't seen him that fancified since . . . well, since her gala opening. "So what brings you to the neighborhood?"

"I should have called first, but I *was* in the neighborhood, actually," he said, appearing decidedly ill at ease. "I brought you something. I bought it from a street vendor." He withdrew a packet of red licorice shoelaces from his inside coat pocket.

She took them hesitantly, at once warmed by the fact that he remembered one of her more frivolous passions, and suspicious of his motives. "Thank you, I think."

"And I want to show you something." He reached inside his other pocket and extracted an envelope. "The slides from the jewelry shoot. I thought you might want copies for your portfolio.''

Halley laughed as she made her way to the light table in the corner of her office. ''In case you hadn't noticed, Jay, I haven't kept up a modeling portfolio in years. I don't plan to make a comeback, either, no matter how good these are.'' She turned on the switch, and the glass table winked to fluorescent life.

Jay laid the ten transparencies side by side on the table. ''The agency's portfolio, then.''

Halley examined the slides one by one, using a magnifying glass. Jay watched her, rocking back and forth on his heels in a manner that told her he was nervous. What did her opinion matter, after all? she wondered.

''They're beautiful, Jay. I mean it. These are some of the best photos ever taken of me.''

He smiled unabashedly. ''Which one do you like best?''

She glanced back at the array of slides, then pointed to two on the end. ''These, in the black dress,'' she said without hesitation. ''It's too bad I didn't discover that dress a little earlier. I could have worn it for all the shots.''

''You don't know how happy I am to hear you say that.''

''Why?'' she asked, her suspicions aroused again.

''Because the client wants them reshot—with the black dress.'' Jay made it sound as if he were delivering a death sentence.

''But I...'' She halted, battling with at least a dozen conflicting responses.

''I explained to the client that you posed for those pictures as a favor,'' Jay said before she could finish her sentence. ''I told him you weren't available for a second sitting.''

''And what did he say?'' she asked, her toe tapping unconsciously against the white carpet as she waited for the other shoe to drop.

"He insisted."

"But couldn't another model—"

Jay was already shaking his head. "It's you he wants. And he's willing to pay for your services."

Halley shivered inside. It wasn't that she didn't want to help Jay out with this dilemma. This jewelry account obviously was an important one to him, and she still owed him, after all. But the thought of the two of them in that studio, with her in that hardly-there dress, and the memory of what Jay's concentrated gaze could do to her—well, the scene just didn't bear repeating.

A refusal was on the tip of her tongue when Jay pulled a business card out of his wallet and handed it to her. "If you don't want to, just say so," he said. "But here's your cut if we reshoot."

Halley's eyes swam when she saw the amount scribbled on the back of the card. "Why would he pay so much just for a model?"

"He liked what he saw. And he can afford it, believe me."

She continued to stare at the staggering figure. Not bad for a few hours' work, and it wasn't as if she didn't need the money. Yet it wasn't the money that lured her into agreeing, against her better judgment. It was the red licorice.

She returned the card to him decisively. "Okay, I'll do it. I'm in no position to turn down good money," she added hastily, since it made a convenient excuse. Then she said, almost as an afterthought, "Will Peg be helping us out?"

"Yeah, sure," he replied, nodding vigorously. "The shoot will go much faster if she's there to help."

Good answer, Jay, she mused silently. "I can do it tomorrow or Friday evening," she said aloud.

"Friday," he agreed. "I really appreciate this, Hal. You're helping me keep a profitable client."

She shrugged. "It's the least I could do. Is baked chicken all right for dinner?"

He smiled, and the sudden warmth in his gaze seemed to bathe her in sunshine. "Chicken is great." He turned abruptly, and with a quick "See you tonight," made a dash for the exit—before she could change her mind about the shoot.

Halley sauntered back to her desk, wondering just what she'd gotten herself into. For crying out loud, a man puts on a tie and gives her licorice, and suddenly she's a glob of clay to be molded to his wishes.

She didn't *want* to pose for Jay, she thought as she absently opened the candy package and extracted one licorice shoelace. She could still vividly recall that achy desire that had sprung to life in the studio last week, and she couldn't risk a repeat performance.

The sparks that had flared so strongly between them were only the result of a flashback, she told herself firmly. The scenario had reminded them of a time when she was still just a model, when they still loved each other with no complications.

They were never more in love than during those first two years, when Jay had followed her rise as a model with constant approval and encouragement. She had told him often enough that she didn't intend to make modeling a long-term career, that she needed to be more than a pretty face pushing a product, but he hadn't seemed to take her seriously. He'd been as much in love with her image as with her and had been quite content with the status quo.

He'd been shocked when she announced her decision to become an agent. He hadn't actually expressed open disapproval and had even seemed supportive, once he got used to the idea. But his lack of confidence in her venture had been obvious, evidenced by his constant attempts to second-guess her decisions and to out-and-out do things for her. If he wasn't trying to invest his money in her company, he was pushing business consultants on her, finding em-

ployees for her, telling her how to set up her photo studio—
and treating her like an incompetent.

She hadn't wanted or needed to be patronized by the sort
of support Jay wanted to give. It reminded her too much of
how her father had "helped" her mother start a business
and the trouble that had caused. To this day she felt the repercussions of that fiasco.

Perhaps more important, however, was that the Mystique Agency was something she had needed to do on her
own, to prove to the world—and maybe to herself—that she
wasn't just a vacuous, empty-headed bimbo who could look
pretty for the camera.

There was no use going over old ground, she told herself
as she returned reluctantly to the depressing task of accounting, still chewing vigorously on the half-eaten licorice
lace. But her eyes blurred as she stared at the numbers
dancing across the page. She and Jay could not go back to
that simpler time, when they loved with such purity, no
strings attached. If she intended to go through with the
photo session, she would do well to remember that.

On any other day, Halley probably would have developed a supreme case of the jitters over her upcoming shoot
with Jay, but Friday provided her with no time to even think
about it. She spent most of the morning in an intense business meeting, emerging from the conference room victo-
rious. A top clothing manufacturer she'd been working on
for months had finally come around, agreeing to an exclu-
sive contract with the agency.

She'd celebrated by buying a magnum of champagne—
domestic, of course, since she was still counting pennies.
She'd hardly popped the cork before she received another
unexpected windfall. A top model, the cream of New York's
finest crop, had severed relations with her former agent and
was now crying on Halley's doorstep, practically begging for

representation. Halley had spent most of the afternoon closeted with the twenty-four-year-old Svetlana, delicately treading the fine line between sympathetic mentor and hard-nosed saleswoman. By four-thirty they had come to terms, and the paperwork was already in motion.

She was still riding high, her euphoria enhanced by champagne, when she breezed into Jay's studio at close to six o'clock. Jay and Peg were already preparing for the shoot, repositioning the lights.

"Guess what?" she asked breathlessly after they'd both called out a greeting.

"You won the lottery?" Jay abandoned his task and focused his attention on her, closing the distance between them.

"Better. I got the Cyndi-O Sportswear account. I've been working on it since—"

"I know, since last summer," Jay finished for her. He was smiling broadly. "That's quite a coup, congratulations." He started to open his arms for a hug, then seemed to think better of it, grasping her hand instead.

Halley searched his face for some small measure of sarcasm, or a sign that the smile was forced, but she found none. In the past she'd often come home bubbling over with some good news, only to meet with Jay's bland response. At best he would offer uneasy congratulations. Tonight he seemed genuinely pleased with her success.

By the time she realized he was still holding her hand, it was too late to extract it gracefully. He stared at her expectantly, as if waiting to hear more. His blue eyes held her ridiculously mesmerized. It must be that cheap champagne, she thought.

"That's great news, Halley," Peg piped in as she joined them, thankfully breaking the spell. "They do a lot of flashy print work, don't they?"

Halley nodded her head as Jay released her hand. "They sure do. And I've got them in the bag. All they have to do is sign on the bottom line. Oh, and I got a new model today, none other than Svetlana."

"Svetlana with the unpronounceable last name?" Jay asked, just as Peg asked, "Wasn't she on the cover of three different fashion magazines last month?"

"Yes and yes," Halley replied exuberantly. "All in all not a bad day. And I couldn't have done it without..." She cast a nervous glance at Peg, who quickly found something requiring her attention on the other side of the studio.

Jay watched her expectantly, waiting for her to complete the sentence.

"I couldn't have held on without your help."

"Despite my meddling?" he teased, warmed by her sudden gratitude. Halley didn't offer thanks all that often, mostly because she seldom allowed herself to be in a position where gratitude was appropriate.

"Even if you were meddling, I was a bit of an ingrate," she said with a self-conscious grin.

"Don't worry about it. You've already returned the favor by agreeing to come here tonight. You really saved my bacon." But even as he shrugged off her thanks, he acknowledged the internal glow she'd just given him. Putting up with her obstinacy and her fury had all been worth it for this moment.

"I'll always help if I can," she returned smoothly. "Now if we can get this shoot wrapped up, I can go to sleep tonight with a smile on my face."

Jay knew all too well what could put a smile on her face late at night, and the thought sobered him. He cleared his throat to mask his sudden discomfort. "The set is ready for you, and the infamous black dress is hanging in the dressing room, cleaned and pressed."

"Oh, thanks, but I brought my own this time," she said, patting the garment bag draped over her shoulder. "It's almost exactly the same style," she added just as Jay was about to object, "but it fits me better. You'll see."

He watched her turn and retreat to the dressing room at a confident, hip-swinging gait. He was glad to see some measure of her self-assuredness return. He was ashamed to admit that at first he'd sort of enjoyed her plight—not because he liked to see her suffer, but because she had finally been forced to acknowledge that she was not Superwoman, and that she needed a helping hand now and again just like everyone else. But seeing her so strung out and worried, day after day, had gnawed away at him. Without any conscious decision on his part, her troubles had become his. He was truly relieved to see things turning around for her.

"What are you staring at?" Peg asked with a cocky grin.

Jay realized he had continued to gaze in the direction of the dressing room, long after Halley had disappeared. He shook his head and turned to face his partner. "Sometimes I get this odd feeling, like I'm seeing Halley for the first time. Do you think she's changed?"

"She seems like the same Halley to me," Peg replied flippantly.

Maybe so, Jay thought. Maybe Halley was the same, and it was what he saw, or what he chose to see, that had changed. He'd once believed her solely responsible for the disintegration of their marriage. *She* was too independent, too self-sufficient. *She* refused to share her problems with him. *She* insisted on rigidly separate careers, separate bank accounts, instead of allowing them to be full life partners. That's how he'd seen things.

In retrospect, he had to take some of the blame. Perhaps *he* had demanded too much of her, more than she was willing—or obligated—to share. Was it so wrong for her to have something all her own, something off limits to him? Perhaps *he* had been too condescending. And there were times, he recalled, when she had wanted to talk, to share something, and he had closed her out.

Maybe he was finally starting to see Halley for who she was, rather than trying to see her as some crazy ideal that she never was, and could never be.

"Ah, what the hell," he muttered. The fact of the matter was that he wanted her, and he was trying to rationalize his desire. But no matter how he looked at it, he and Halley were divorced, and wanting her was just plain useless. If he was going to do any soul-searching, he should have done it long before now.

"I forgot to ask, did you want my hair up or down?"

Jay turned sharply to be greeted by the vision of a goddess. Now he remembered the dress, a black silk number by a prominent designer. It was similar to the other dress, as she'd promised, but infinitely classier. She'd worn it for the gala opening at her new office. At the time he hadn't fully appreciated it, the way it accentuated her breasts and clung seductively to her willowy figure. No, that night he'd been plagued by thoughts of a much more bitter nature.

"Jay?"

He realized he hadn't answered her question. "Start with your hair up," he said, envisioning the long, slender column of her neck. "You can always take it down later." Or he could take it down, letting the dark, silky waves fall over his hands, as they had when he'd massaged her shoulders....

But of course he wouldn't touch her. That was the only sane choice.

The session went smoothly enough, Jay thought, from a technical point of view. He and Halley had already worked out the bugs during the last shoot, figuring out the nuances of each pose, so that the process moved along at a fast clip.

On a more personal level, however, he found the evening excruciating.

All those nights sharing a roof with Halley, knowing she was in the next bedroom but unable to touch her, had pushed Jay well past a strong man's tolerance level, and right now he didn't feel all that strong.

Thank God Peg was here. Thank God... "Peg?" he called out, suddenly realizing she wasn't there at all.

"She went to answer the phone," Halley supplied. "Didn't you hear it ring?"

"Guess not," he answered after taking a deep, calming breath. He had been so preoccupied with Halley that the building could have fallen down around them and he probably wouldn't have noticed.

"Do you need something?" Halley asked innocently.

She had to ask, he thought, gritting his teeth. "No, nothing." He peered through the viewfinder once more, intent on finishing this job if it was the last thing he did—and it just might be. Could a man die from an overdose of willpower?

When he heard Peg's footsteps returning to the set, he relaxed somewhat. As long as they had a chaperon, the temptation remained one firmly out of reach.

"Who was that?" he asked casually, snapping off a shot.

"That was the very delectable man I went out with last week. He invited me to his apartment for a cappuccino," she explained as she fastened her cape. "So I'm afraid I'll have to—"

"You're leaving?" Jay and Halley both shot the question toward Peg at the same time.

Peg looked at first one, then the other. "Yes, I'm leaving," she reassured them. "Believe me, this guy doesn't have to ask twice... what's wrong with you two? You've almost got this shoot wrapped up. You don't really need me hanging around and getting in the way, do you?"

You have no idea how much, Jay thought. But he couldn't think of a single logical reason, other than the truth, to keep her here. "Well," he hedged, looking hopefully at Halley. Didn't she need something? A fresh application of lipstick or powder? But no, her appearance was perfect. And she obviously couldn't think of an excuse, either, though she looked every bit as panicked as he felt. "Well, I guess we can manage without you," he muttered.

"Great, then I'll see you Monday," Peg said as she checked her fly-away hair in the mirror on the wall. "Halley, it was nice seeing you again. Don't let the Swede here work you too hard."

"No, I won't," she answered limply.

In the matter of a few seconds they were alone.

Halley was once again wearing the jeweled headpiece and ankle bracelet, assuming the bare-legged, chin-on-knees pose that had provided such fantastic results last week. The black silk was draped provocatively around her thighs.

"How's this?" she asked.

"Sexy," he answered automatically, and very sincerely.

"Too sexy?" she asked. "I mean, am I showing too much?"

"No, dammit, you look perfect, okay?" His words came out sounding strained and impatient, which he immediately regretted as Halley flinched. He turned away from her, rubbing his forehead as he tried to reclaim his bearings.

"Then what's wrong?" she asked, responding to his unwarranted spurt of anger with softness and understanding, something he didn't deserve.

"Nothing!" He sliced out the word as if it were a machete. "I broke my concentration. Just give me a minute, all right?"

"Sorry," she murmured.

"Don't apologize. You didn't do anything." *Except what you do naturally,* he added silently.

"I thought maybe something was wrong with the dress," she said, still to his back.

Even as his body hardened, Jay felt his attitude soften. She didn't deserve his antagonism. Still, keeping a bit of anger between them sounded like the most effective method for thwarting the desire.

He marshaled his wits and returned his attention to the camera, though merely photographing her loveliness was a distinctly unfulfilling prospect, given the other possibilities . . . *im*possibilities, he reminded himself.

"No, you look beautiful, the dress is stunning. Unfortunately all I can think about is how good you would look out of it." The words escaped before he could stop them. He braced himself for an angry response, knowing he deserved it. He was way out of line.

It didn't come.

"I see," she said, dragging the words out. "Does that mean the shoot is over for the day?"

"No," he answered decisively, calling upon what little professionalism he could muster at the moment. "No, we have to finish this. If we don't, you'll have to come back, and frankly I can't handle another evening like this."

As he turned to face her, she appeared all business. "I agree," she said coolly, repositioning herself on the carpeted platform, striking the now well-practiced pose and come-hither expression.

Jay took one look through the camera, groaned, and threw up his hands. "Forget it. Let's just forget it."

"Now what's wrong?"

"You're not going on any brochure looking like...like..."

"Like what?" she shot back, her voice high-pitched with frustration.

"Like you're about to strip off that dress and make love. I don't think you want every man in New York to see you like that!"

"Maybe I look that way because it's exactly how I feel."

In the silence that followed, every muscle in Jay's body rearranged itself in surprise. Did she mean...he didn't dare hope, and yet...

He moved away from the camera and came toward her, one slow step at a time, as he studied the play of expressions on her face. Though she never broke her pose, her blue-green eyes were riveted on his every move, revealing more than even her words had.

He stopped an arm's length away from her, debating as to whether he should close the short remaining distance between them. The last time he'd kissed Halley he'd almost gotten himself slapped. She had given him fair warning, after all, that if he again took advantage of any situation, she'd let him have it regardless of who was to blame. Knowing Halley, he didn't doubt her for a minute.

He stuck his hands in his jeans pockets to keep from reaching for her. "I want you, Halley, and you seem to want me. What do you think we should do about it?"

"Control ourselves?" she suggested, though not very forcefully.

He considered that option for a moment and found it totally unappealing. He gave her a look that said so. "Are you sure?"

She nodded. "We would be very foolish to act on impulse," she said, uncurling herself from the pose and swinging her legs over the side of the platform.

"You're right, of course. We have to be practical."

"Sensible," she agreed, smiling faintly. "I mean, what would be the point of sharing a night of mindless passion when we obviously have no future?"

"A wasted effort," he said, matching her smile.

"You're a rotten liar," she said, turning suddenly serious.

He reached out a hand to smooth her hair, the gesture a request he could not put into words. How could he verbalize the ways he longed to worship her body, and then claim it for his own, to possess and be possessed? He wanted a fusion of flesh and minds and souls that went far beyond the carnal aspects of sex. He wanted that rare closeness that only two people who joined in such a way could have, even if it was only for a night.

She closed her eyes and turned her face toward his hand, brushing her lips against his palm. "Jay," she whispered. The single utterance, so full of pain and longing, was the answer he needed to hear.

In one fluid movement she was in his arms, their mouths joined in passion. He held her tightly, as if she might evaporate, while his mouth plundered hers in an ungentle manner. Tonight he doubted whether he was a gentleman at all.

Halley was no more tame than he. She welcomed his rough embrace, her hands tangled in his hair and pulling— pulling as if she could bring him closer that way.

Jay could think of several dozen ways to bring them closer, and he wanted to try as many as possible. He intended to draw out this evening any way he could, for he had no guarantee of a repeat performance. It seemed an eternity since he'd held her like this, and his body was already impatient for completion. But he could and would control his own yearning, in favor of Halley's.

Like the initial blaze of a match, their frantic passion eased into a steady burning. Their kisses slowed, becoming more leisurely. At last they paused to simply hold each other. Jay buried his face in her hair, inhaling the lightly perfumed scent of it. "You look like pure sin in that dress, you know," he said, caressing the silk at the small of her back and over her hips. "But I'd still like to see you out of it."

"And you will," Halley returned in a throaty whisper. "The moment we get home."

"Home?" The word carried a certain note of wicked amusement. "If you think I'm waiting till we get home, you're sadly mistaken."

Her eyes widened. "Just where do you intend to—oh!" He'd scooped her up and was carrying her determinedly toward the office. "Not that awful couch!" But she couldn't help laughing. The gold velour couch in his office—some long-ago decorator's mortal sin—had provided them with quite a few entertaining evenings during their brief courtship, hard springs and all.

"You'll see," Jay said, nudging the office door open with his foot. He flipped on the light with his elbow, then set her down, as gently as he would a Dresden doll, on a gorgeous blue-gray tweed sofa.

"You redecorated," she said, surprised.

"Quite some time ago. You haven't been here for a while. But I didn't bring you in here to talk about interior design." He gave her a meaningful smile as he extinguished the light once more. A soft city glow illuminated them through the single window. He sat down on the couch beside her and seemingly in no hurry, took off his shoes, then his pullover sweater. Halley waited breathlessly.

Suddenly, without preamble, he pulled her into his lap.

She nestled against his hard chest as his lips sought hers once again. His kiss, at once tender and demanding, sent waves of pleasure shimmering into every part of her. His tongue darted against hers, withdrew, then returned in an exciting game. The kissing was only a prelude, she mused headily, of more exciting games to come. The prospect filled her mind and stole away her breath. The lovemaking she and Jay created was never matter-of-fact.

As they kissed, his hand slid under the hem of her gown and made a casual exploration of her bare ankle, her calf, her knee. With every inch of progress he made along her leg, Halley shivered with anticipation. While he teased her inner thigh with one hand, his other found the zipper at the back of her dress and gently eased it down. The black silk slid to Halley's waist, revealing her breasts to Jay's feral gaze.

The desire so plainly reflected in his eyes warmed her. With a welcoming smile she took his hand and placed it over her breast. Not that he was shy or needed encouragement, but she ached for the feel of his skin against hers. The intimate contact made her head spin.

"Oh, baby," was all he could say.

Baby. *Baby!* She flew into a sitting position, combating a wave of panic. How could she be so stupid and careless? "Oh, Jay, I just thought of something awful. Truly dreadful."

He drew his hand away as if he'd been burned. "What? My God, Halley, what?"

"When I was in Paris?"

"Yes?" he prompted.

"I ran out of my birth control pills and I . . . I just never got them refilled. There was no need." She shrugged apologetically, bracing herself for his reaction. She ought to be jailed for letting things progress this far when she couldn't possibly see them through.

He surprised her by smiling indulgently. "You had me worried. I thought it was something really bad." He surprised her further by dipping his head and placing his warm, moist mouth firmly over her left breast.

She gasped, her fingernails digging into his shoulder, as his tongue made lazy circles around her nipple. "Jay!"

Seemingly unconcerned, he transferred his attentions to her other breast.

"If you'd just . . . stop that I could . . ." The sentence degenerated into a moan. Oh, he could make her feel so *good*.

Whatever he did, whatever part of her anatomy he chose to honor, he could set her whole body on fire.

He gave a low chuckle as he pushed her playfully back onto the cushions, then leaned over her until his soft cotton shirt brushed against her taut breasts. "Is there a problem?" he asked as he nuzzled her ear.

"We have no birth control, Casanova," she said, firmly pushing him away. "And if you have a solution to that problem hidden in your desk drawer, I'll wonder just exactly what you do all those evenings you work late."

He laughed again. "No, I'm afraid I don't have an immediate solution." He trailed a finger between her breasts, down her stomach, and to her navel, which was about where the black dress had stalled on its way off her body.

"You seem awfully cavalier about this."

He smiled wickedly. "You know as well as I do there are ways around such a dilemma."

She certainly did, and her pulse raced a little faster just thinking about them.

He teased her flat abdomen with his fingertips. "The first time we were together, we had a similar problem, remember?"

She nodded, feeling the blush rise in her face. The things he had done to her that night, the things they'd done to each other, had been delightfully shocking to the naive Pennsylvania country girl she'd been. And all without any risk of pregnancy. But tonight she wanted—needed—more. She needed the ultimate closeness of having him inside her. "What if we want to make love?" she objected.

He laughed that devilish laugh again. "That's for dessert." With one quick, almost magically skilled movement, he whisked the black dress over Halley's hips, down her legs and off, revealing the ridiculously skimpy scrap of silk she called underwear. He gave a low whistle of appreciation. "I'm still working on the appetizers."

Six

———

Halley tensed, then melted as he kissed her again. His hands seemed to be everywhere at once—in her hair, caressing her breasts, trailing white-hot paths along her legs. Her mind wanted to resist, insisting it wasn't wise to allow a man who set her afire to remove her clothing when she wasn't protected. But deep down she knew she could trust Jay to be responsible.

With that comforting thought she sighed and happily let go of all control, allowing him to pleasure her as only he could. She realized, as he teased her navel with his tongue, that she was almost naked while he was still fully clothed. She opened her mouth to object, but somehow she didn't have the energy to equalize the situation. The rivers of heat coursing through her veins paralyzed her with pleasure.

When he exhausted every possibility with her navel, he slipped his fingers beneath the lace waistband of her panties and freed her of the silk barrier. As if from a distance, she heard his sharp intake of breath, and she knew that he wasn't as masterfully in control as he'd like her to think. She smiled with purely feminine delight.

His lips found her again, this time nibbling their way across her hip bone and down to her thigh. His kisses became light as snowflakes, interspersed with teasing nips that went up and down in maddening little trails, moving inexorably closer to the nest of curls at the juncture of her legs.

Halley knew exactly what he had in mind, and she was about to faint with the anticipation. "Don't torture me, Jay," she pleaded.

He made no answer, continuing his sweet ministrations at a leisurely pace despite her protests. When at last he parted her legs and softly kissed the source of her womanly pleasure, she did die a little as a jolt of volcanic heat seemed to electrify her every nerve ending.

The more she wiggled, the more intense his loving assault became. The river of pleasure rose higher, more powerful, pushing against an ever-weakening dam until the pressure was too great. A flood tide crashed through the wall, and Halley felt herself splinter into a thousand fragments of shimmering warmth.

When some measure of sanity returned, she could still hear the echoes of her own cries of ecstasy ringing in her ears. Jay held her, squeezing her tight against his chest and rocking her back and forth.

"This is a tad one-sided, don't you think?" she murmured, touching his smooth jaw. She wondered if he'd shaved for her, and how and when he'd done it.

"Not at all."

"But I'm not wearing a stitch and you've hardly begun to undress. Something's not quite balanced about that."

"I'm not complaining," he said, winding a tendril of her hair around his finger. "You have no idea how exciting you are, and how much it pleases me that I can reduce you to quivering incoherence."

"Well, I *am* complaining," she argued cheerfully, "ungracious as that may sound. 'Quivering incoherence' doesn't say much for my seduction technique."

"You don't need a technique," he replied huskily. "All you need is that black dress."

"You hated that dress when I first bought it."

"I hated the price tag. I know, I know, don't say it," he said when she started to object. "The money didn't come out of my pocket, so why should I care? I don't, not anymore. That wasn't really the issue anyway, you know."

"What was the issue?" she asked.

"If I promise to tell you later, can we not talk about it now?"

She smiled, running her hands down the front of his shirt. "Deal. I can think of *much* better things to concern ourselves with." She toyed with his shirt buttons, but he grabbed her wrists and stilled her efforts.

"Let's go home," he said, nuzzling her ear.

"I suggested that an hour ago."

"Aren't you glad I didn't listen?"

She was, she thought as she scampered back to the dressing room and threw her clothes on willy-nilly, stuffing the silk dress into its garment bag with little thought to treating it gently. By the time Jay had packaged the evening's film and shut down the lights, she was already wrapped in her fox coat and standing by the door, impatient to be gone.

At that time of night taxis seldom frequented the narrow street in the Gramercy Park area where Jay's warehouse studio stood, so they set out for the long walk home. A light snow was falling—seems they'd had a lot of snow the past few weeks—but the wind was still, so it wasn't particularly cold.

Though he hadn't said so, Jay had been afraid that once they got outside in the cold air, Halley's normal caution would return, and what had seemed an inevitable encounter might suddenly become precipitous in her eyes. But the intimacy they'd so recently created remained with them as they strolled arm in arm, with soft snowflakes hitting their faces and collecting on their sleeves and in their hair.

They stopped at an all-night drugstore, where Halley, her face burning with embarrassment, perused the candy aisle while Jay took care of their "dilemma." She laughed into her collar when they returned to the street, as if they were teenagers preparing for an illicit adventure.

As they crossed from Gramercy into the Village, they stopped under an old-fashioned street lamp for the traffic to clear. Jay looked down at Halley, at her flushed, expectant face, and felt an overwhelming wave of emotion.

She used to be his, and now she wasn't, he thought, stinging with regret. The loss had never come home to him so sharply as it did at that moment, when they were closer then they'd been in months.

"Jay, what's wrong?" Halley asked, her forehead wrinkled in concern. "You look . . . strange."

In answer he kissed her, his mouth hard and possessive on hers. She wasn't his wife anymore, but she was his for this night, and he wanted her to understand that.

Halley didn't seem inclined to argue. The moment they were through the front door, she dropped her purse and garment bag on the floor in the entryway and quickly shrugged out of her coat as Jay did the same. They both pulled off their snowboots and kicked them aside.

Then she stood in front of him and looked up with a solemn face. "Bedroom. Now. I would sweep you up and carry you there if I could, but I'm afraid I'd rupture something."

Jay was all too willing to comply, following her lead. He had just thrown the paper sack from the drugstore onto the bed when Halley launched an energetic campaign of her own. She pushed him down onto the mattress and draped herself over him.

"You despicable rogue," she breathed, stretching to kiss both corners of his mouth. "How dare you flaunt your considerable influence over my body without letting me return the favor." She stopped to kiss him full on the mouth, invading aggressively with her tongue. "Well, turnabout's fair play, you know. You may have served up the appetizer, but the main course is all mine."

"We'll see about that," he said through a chuckle as she made quick work of his shirt buttons. She issued an unladylike curse when she couldn't get the cuff buttons undone. He soothed her as he helped out, which only inflamed her more.

"Stop wiggling," she commanded as she tried to disengage him from his undershirt.

"It's hard not to wiggle when I'm about to explode," he explained patiently, if a bit raggedly. "So if you don't hurry things along, I might just have to take over."

"Ha!" she retorted, leaning her cheek against his bare chest for a brief moment. She flicked his nipple with her tongue, just once, before turning her attention to the buttons on his jeans. He gritted his teeth as her strong, capable hands unwittingly—or maybe not so unwittingly—drove him crazy. He had shown major self-control during his seduction of her, but that control was fast leaving him.

Once she had him divested of all his clothing, she made him wait while she performed a leisurely striptease. There was just enough light from the hallway to illuminate her sleek silhouette.

"Sure you don't need help?" he asked, gripping the sheets in tight fists.

"No, but you will when I get done with you," she teased. When she took her place beside him, however, the teasing was gone from her voice. "Oh, Jay, I need this so much. No more games. Make love to me. Just hold me and love me—" She buried her face against his neck.

He held her for a few moments, stroking her back, almost overcome with tenderness for her. "That's all I want, too," he murmured, running his hands across her smooth flesh, down her hip and between her legs. She moaned when he caressed her there. She was more than ready for him, and he was definitely overdue for her.

He was nearly out of his mind with desire by the time he'd taken care of the necessary precaution. When he turned back to Halley, she parted her long legs in welcome, eager for their union. He settled himself between them, still attempting to draw out their pleasure, but at her urgent plea he imbedded himself in her warmth with one quick thrust.

She sighed with delight. He groaned at the exquisite pleasure. He would have liked to prolong the ecstasy, but at this point he held his control by only a thread.

Thankfully Halley wasn't of a mind to tarry, either. She pushed against him and they established a frantic rhythm, accelerating straight up to a dizzying peak. Just when he thought he couldn't stand it a moment longer, he felt her tighten around him, her climax imminent. That was all the impetus he needed to let go. His cry of pleasure joined hers in a perfectly timed unison that they had seldom achieved, even as seasoned lovers.

It seemed to Jay as if they floated back to earth.

"Don't let me go," Halley whispered . . . or did he only imagine that she spoke?

"I've got you," he answered anyway, gathering her into his arms. He held her for a long time, until the room had stopped spinning and their breathing had slowed to normal.

"I really blew it," Halley commented idly.

"What? Not in my book. No way."

"Still, you outclass me when it comes to running the show. The little bit of control I took—I gave it right back to you as soon as the going got tough." She sighed and snuggled closer.

"Does that bother you?"

She gave him a throaty laugh. "Do I look bothered?"

"No, you look thoroughly satisfied to me."

She reached down and pinched his behind. "Don't be so smug."

"How about tomorrow morning? How will you feel then?" He hated to bring it up. But he wanted fair warning if she intended to wake up in an unreasonable mood about all this.

"Mmm . . . we *are* going to have to deal with this little indiscretion in the cold light of day, aren't we." She paused, and when she resumed speaking, her voice was smaller than usual, timid, almost. "But let's not think about it till then, okay?"

"Okay." That suited him fine.

She fell asleep soon afterward, but Jay lay awake for a long time. "Oh, baby, what am I going to do with you?" he asked the darkness.

Halley awoke sometime before dawn. She was curled up with her back against Jay's chest, warm and secure, and she sighed with contentment. It was only as she came more fully awake that she realized something was wrong with this picture, and she remembered exactly what had happened last night.

Without moving she looked out the window and noted the first streaks of light in the gray sky. *The cold light of day.* Here it comes, she thought grimly. She'd better sort a few things out in her mind.

She scooted away from Jay, immediately regretting the loss of warmth, but she could not think clearly while remaining so close to him. She didn't go far, just to the chintz easy chair a few feet from the bed. She covered herself with an afghan and tucked her feet under her, preparing herself for a long, hard look at what she'd done.

Surprisingly, she felt no guilt, no regret. How could she when even now, as she gazed on Jay's masculine form snuggled under the blankets, she wanted to go to him? Last night was nothing short of delicious as they'd remembered their shared passions. What was more, through their physical closeness they had opened the door for further communication. She sensed a new receptiveness in Jay, and perhaps a new willingness in herself to listen and be more frank. They'd had precious little frankness before the divorce.

The divorce. Now that was something they couldn't ignore. When they had decided to officially end their marriage, it seemed there was no other alternative. Had anything really changed since then? Or was she merely looking at things through the rose-tinted glasses of recent intimacy?

The divorce was a done deed, after all. They couldn't go back and undo it ... or could they? If a marriage could be undone, so could a divorce, she supposed.

But she was way ahead of herself. One step at a time. She would have to test the waters first, see if Jay was even of a mind to discuss the things that had driven them apart and work toward eliminating them. Until then, she had no intention of simply taking up where they left off, sexually speaking. It would be all too easy to assume a semi-permanent place in Jay's bed and pretend, for a while, that all was peachy keen. But as long as their relationship was in limbo—whatever *kind* of a relationship theirs was—last night would have to be put into perspective. It was a glorious interlude, an opening, a stepping stone. It certainly didn't represent the new status quo.

She chewed nervously on her bottom lip. She hoped Jay would understand that.

She wouldn't have to wait long to find out. He was already stirring, growing restless. He reached a hand out to the empty space Halley had so recently vacated, and when he found nothing, he grabbed onto her pillow and pulled it to his chest, inhaling deeply. The subconscious gesture touched her.

She should leave, make some coffee, take a shower—put on clothes. But she didn't do any of those things. Instead she sat and watched Jay as the room grew brighter.

At last he opened his eyes and focused them on Halley. "What are you doing all the way over there?" he asked, his voice still heavy with sleep.

"Just thinking," she answered.

"It's not the cold light of day yet, is it?" He gave her a questioning half smile that curled her toes.

"Pretty soon," she returned.

He gave the room a calculating once-over. "Not for another hour," he declared. "Come back to bed."

She did.

"You're awfully quiet," Jay commented as he poured himself a second cup of coffee. He and Halley were showered and dressed, a far cry from the rumpled, earthy lovers who had reluctantly parted company an hour ago, but he supposed that was a good thing. If they were to have any sort of meaningful talk this morning—and he had a feeling that was on the agenda—they needed some distance, physical and emotional, from what they'd just experienced together.

"I'm still just thinking," she responded. "And you? Are you thinking?"

He nodded. "Regrets?"

She shook her head. "None having to do with last night."
She could have put an inviting tease in her words, but she
didn't. In fact, she appeared formidably serious, seated
ramrod straight at the breakfast bar with her black coffee in
front of her. Not hostile, just serious.

He stood in the kitchen across from her, absently sorting
the silverware he'd just taken out of the dishwasher. "What
did it mean to you? Last night, that is." Might as well jump
in with both feet, he figured.

She pulled at her lower lip with her teeth. "Can we start
with an easier question?"

"Like what?" he asked amiably.

She thought for a moment. "The black dress. You said
the price wasn't the reason you were so...miffed that first
time I wore it, and you promised to talk about it later. Well,
it's later. What *did* put you in such a lousy mood the night
of my party?"

"That's easy?" Jay took a sobering sip of his coffee. He'd
always heard that promises made in the midst of lovemaking had a way of coming back to haunt a man. The words
he'd been glib with last night stuck in his throat this morning.

"All right then, I'll begin," Halley said. "Every time I
think about the night of my gala opening I get a sick feeling
in the pit of my stomach."

"You do?"

"It was supposed to be a big evening for me, an important step for my business," she explained in a carefully detached voice, "and I really wanted to share the excitement
with you. I had this great dress, I worked an hour on my
hair, and then you..." Her voice trailed off.

"And then I acted like a jerk," he said without hesitation.

She flashed an uneasy smile. "I didn't want to come out
and say it quite that way, but you weren't what I would call

supportive. You abandoned me. You stood at the bar all night and drank scotch with that Ford model—a *Ford* model! Jay, you could have at least picked one of mine. That really hurt.'' She no longer sounded detached.

''I had the impression you didn't need me at all,'' he countered. ''You were in your element, showing off your new digs, displaying all your hot new models like trophies, courting the press, posing for photographers. You were a star that night. I was...I don't know. Out of place, I guess. I felt more like an accessory than a husband.''

''Congratulations. Now you know how a model feels— how I felt around you and your colleagues sometimes, when all I had going for me was a photogenic face.'' She stopped herself and frowned into her coffee. ''The way I acted that night—it was all for show, you know, all the posturing and smiling. I couldn't very well tell everyone to cool their heels while I chased you around the room, trying to get you to tell me what was wrong besides my dress being too expensive.''

He rolled his eyes. ''Come on, Halley, you weren't thinking about me that night.''

''I thought about you through every minute of that whole grim affair,'' she said firmly. ''No matter how cheerful and confident I looked, I was miserable, because for the first time I was forced to admit that something was wrong—very wrong—between us and I was scared to death.''

Jay didn't know quite how to respond. Halley, scared? He'd never heard her talk like this before. He'd had no idea, in fact, that his rotten attitude that night had made any impression on her at all.

''I was jealous,'' he muttered, rattling the silverware and half-hoping she didn't hear him.

''Jealous?'' she repeated in a bewildered tone.

''*Envious* is a better word. Here you were in this luxurious new office that put mine to shame, wearing a dress I couldn't have afforded to buy for you, with a dozen reporters and another dozen clients I would die for hanging on your every word . . . I guess it just got to me, that's all."

He chanced a look at her. She'd gone all soft and dewy, but she didn't say anything.

"I should have brought all this up two years ago," he continued. "It's a little late to apologize."

"But I am sorry I made you feel so—"

"No, no, not you. Me. It's too late for me to apologize for ruining your evening. Anyway, I'd like to talk about something a little more recent."

"Oh, yes. Last night," she said, accepting the change of subject gracefully.

"And this morning," he reminded her. "You're sure you don't regret it?"

She grinned. "Of course I'm sure. Listen to us. We're talking, at least, and we wouldn't be if we hadn't—well—broken down some barriers last night."

"And this morning," he said again, returning her grin. But then he sobered. "Why do I get the feeling you don't want to make this a regular habit?"

"It's tempting, believe me . . ."

"But?" He knew there was more.

"But think about it," she said, obviously trying to sound practical. "We get all cozy and intimate again, and meanwhile we're talking out all our problems, and . . . and, well, suppose it doesn't work."

She had a point. "We'd have to rip ourselves apart all over again," he said.

"Exactly. I don't know how you feel, but I'm not up to that." There was a definite catch in her voice.

"Me neither. Is this what you've been thinking about so hard?"

She nodded.

"And what do you suggest?"

"Well, for now, I'd like to remain your temporary tenant—in the guest room—and I'll keep looking for an apartment. Beyond that..." She shrugged. "Take things as they come, I guess."

"That sounds prudent. And wise. And not much fun," he grumbled.

She narrowed her eyebrows in a silent warning.

"But I won't argue," he added. This was much, much more than he had hoped for.

The weekend went well, Halley decided as she rode the subway to work Monday morning in a jovial mood. She didn't even mind it when an obviously unwashed man sat next to her and offered a sip from his pint of who-knows-what. She merely smiled and declined, explaining that she had just brushed her teeth.

She couldn't honestly say that she and Jay were headed for a reconciliation, although during weak moments she knew she was wishing for just that. But at least they were talking, if not always amicably.

They had argued several times—that was to be expected. After all, they were bringing up sensitive subjects, opening old wounds that hadn't healed. Halley was discovering hurts she hadn't even known she harbored—things she had pushed to the back of her mind where they festered. But between the arguments, they'd gotten a few things straight. A few, that was a start.

The most astonishing thing Halley had learned was that Jay did in fact see her as a successful business owner. Gradually, grudgingly, he'd come to admit that she knew her stuff and was doing well.

His attempts to become involved with her business weren't always due to an overwhelming macho urge to control or subjugate her, as she'd previously thought. Sometimes Jay simply felt a sense of obligation. As her husband he felt he should share her responsibilities—and accept just a little of the credit. He would never have admitted that a few months ago.

It was a basic male tendency for him to feel needed by his wife. And she'd shut him out, denied him even a tiny piece of her work world, all in the name of independence. Perhaps she'd been too rigid. Suppose she did decide to share more of her professional life with Jay. How did she go about it without the risk of losing control altogether?

Loosening her white-knuckle grip on the agency wouldn't be easy. She could admit that she maintained a slightly exaggerated fear of losing control of her business—her dream. That was only natural, given the example her mother had set for her. Cora Hays had touched her dream, her own little slice of the world, only to have it swept away from her in a heartbeat. And all because she'd placed her trust in someone other than herself.

It's not like sex, she mused with a guilty grin as she thought about their spectacular night together. She had found it so easy to turn the reins over to Jay after their playful tussle for "control." Somehow that attitude just didn't translate into her professional life.

But maybe it could . . . maybe. If she could trust Jay so completely with her body, how was it she couldn't trust him not to hurt her beloved agency? She resolved to work on that. By the time she entered the Korman Building, she had an optimistic spring in her step.

"Good morning!" she called cheerfully as she came through the agency's front doors. But her smile fell flat when she got a look at Kathryn's face. "Oh, no, what now?"

"You obviously haven't read the morning paper," Kathryn answered miserably. "Here." She handed Halley the Lifestyle section. "Cecily's column, page four."

Halley's hands shook as she turned to the popular gossip columnist's daily dose of flash and trash, knowing exactly what she would find. Some vindictive weasel had leaked the news of the Mystique Agency's financial woes.

"That witch!" Halley railed as she read the account. The columnist made her sound like an airhead model who'd grown bored with her easy life and decided to dabble in entrepreneurship, only to be thwarted by the big, bad, real world.

"Cecily conveniently forgets to mention I've been in business for four years," Halley grumbled. "She makes it sound like my success is nothing more than luck, and that I was naive and careless to hire Harold in the first place. Good Lord, the man had credentials as long as my arm and I checked out every one of them before I hired him. How was I supposed to know he'd suddenly turn to embezzling?"

"I know, I know," Kathryn commiserated.

"And this picture of me is grotesque! Where did they dig that one up?" But she stopped raving long enough to read the rest of the column, which made her even more furious. Cecily had learned of Halley's divorce "from dashing and successful commercial photographer Jay Jernigan, now one of New York's most eligible bachelors," and had attempted to tie it in with the agency's fiscal problems—as if Jay were somehow responsible for Halley's previous success and that, without him, she was doomed to failure.

"If that doesn't take the cake," Halley finally said. The irony would almost be amusing, if it weren't so infuriating. After all she'd done to keep Jay *out* of her agency business, the press still wanted to give *him* credit for *her* success. "Isn't this libelous, slanderous . . . something?"

"I already called the lawyer," Kathryn said. "He told me there's really no grounds for legal action."

"Well, hell." Halley folded the paper and returned it to Kathryn's desk, her temper spent for the moment. "We can hope nobody reads the paper today, but I guess that's asking too much." Even as she said this, Kathryn disconnected the answering service and switched on her phone. One line on the console immediately lit up with an incoming call. Halley sighed. "Send all the nasty calls to my office. Looks like I'll be spending my day buried in damage control."

Seven

————

Reaction to the newspaper column was worse than even Halley had anticipated. The phone calls began as a trickle at first, and then a deluge. Models were worried about their images and their futures. Clients were concerned about ongoing contracts. And creditors, damn them, were starting to get antsy about being paid. Even when friends and associates called with legitimate concern, finding Cecily's column hard to believe, Halley was annoyed.

But she never let her annoyance show. She did the same song-and-dance she'd done on that first day, when she'd returned from Europe to find the agency stripped clean. She admitted to financial problems, openly hinting that Cecily had greatly exaggerated. She scraped the bottom of the barrel to find the funds to pay her most overdue bills. And with a smile on her face and in her voice, she assured everyone who would listen that the Mystique Agency would not, under any circumstances, close its doors.

Her overt optimism could only do so much. Predictably the previous week's business coups turned sour as a result of the bad publicity. Svetlana failed to show up at the appointed time to sign her new contract. Halley learned later, through a third party, that the illusive model was having second thoughts. Cyndi-O Sportswear handily pulled out of its commitment.

The IRS called, unable to decipher Halley's garbled explanation as to why the agency hadn't paid its quarterly tax estimate. And then the *coup de grace:* the agency's staff photographer, David Henson, quit without even an hour's notice. He confessed, rather ashamedly, that he'd been offered another position some weeks ago and that he felt it would be wise to make the move to "a more stable company."

The photography studio was just a sideline, anyhow, Halley thought, trying to console herself. She'd found it convenient to have David at her disposal, and she'd managed to generate just enough business, mostly from smaller ad agencies, to make the studio pay for itself. The Mystique Agency could get along without the photo work, but what was she going to do with the jobs that were already scheduled?

She would have to hire a replacement, and that might take time. She thought briefly of sending all the jobs to Jay's studio, then rejected the idea. He was busy enough with his own clients. So she had Kathryn reschedule the photo work to the following week. Hopefully by then Halley would think of something.

Noon brought a brief respite from disaster. Kathryn, bubbling with curiosity, brought a stately arrangement of peach roses into Halley's office, then found excuses to linger as Halley sliced open the tiny blue envelope bearing her name.

A sympathy offering from a catty competitor? Halley wondered as she unfolded the small card. Or was her banker buttering her up before he called in her loan? She soon discovered it was neither when she read the message: "I saw the paper this morning. That's a tough break. Thought you could use a pick-me-up. J."

"Who sent them?" Kathryn demanded point-blank when Halley wasn't forthcoming with an explanation. "Tell me, I'm dying!"

"They're from Jay," she answered, her voice sounding dreamy even to her own ears. "I can't recall that he ever sent me flowers before."

Kathryn sighed. "And roses, too. That's so romantic." She caught herself and turned a shade of red that clashed with her carrot-colored hair. "I mean, it would be romantic if you guys were still...oh Halley, pull my foot out of my mouth, would you?"

Halley laughed. "It's all right, Kath. Roses *are* romantic, just what we need to cheer us up." She extracted one of the larger blooms from the arrangement and handed it to her receptionist. "Here, have some romance. I think you need the pick-me-up more than I do. You're the one who has to answer the phone. Who *is* answering the phone, by the way?"

Kathryn took the hint. With the rose held gingerly between two fingers, she saluted and skittered out of the room.

Still smiling, Halley shook her head as she swept the remains of her deli lunch into the trash. She then positioned the flowers in the center of her desk, making it impossible for her to get any work done. She sat down in her chair, put her chin in her hands, and admired the stunning bouquet.

Jay's gesture certainly was romantic, just as Kathryn had said. But it meant much more to Halley. The flowers were his way of offering his moral support without interfering.

Impulsively she picked up the phone and dialed the number at his warehouse studio.

"Jay-Zee Photography," Jay answered cheerfully, as he always did.

"Thank you," Halley said without introduction.

"You're welcome," he returned, sounding pleased.

"What possessed you?" she couldn't resist asking. "You've never sent me flowers before."

"That's not true. What about our first anniversary?"

Halley searched her memory. "Ah, yes. The schefflera plant. That's not exactly roses, but I guess it qualifies," she teased. "Anyway, once in five years still isn't such a sterling record. I'm not complaining, mind you."

"You really want to know why I sent them?"

At the warning note in his voice, she wasn't at all sure. "Maybe not, but tell me anyway."

"When I saw that column in the paper this morning, my first urge was to drop everything, march down to that newspaper office, and wring Cecily Dawson's neck."

Halley blanched at the thought. "Justifiable homicide," she murmured.

"Maybe so, but it also would have been interfering, jumping into your battle, something I didn't think you'd appreciate."

"No, I probably wouldn't have," she agreed. Finally, *finally*, she was getting through to him.

"I couldn't just sit here. I knew the publicity would cause you some problems and I had to do something to make it easier for you. Flowers...pretty weak consolation, but that was the best I could come up with."

"It was the perfect thing to do," she stated positively. "It's been a horrible morning, I've been grumpy and awful to my whole staff, and now I'm—smiling. Yes, I'm actually smiling as my business goes down the tubes."

"Is it that bad?" he asked warily.

"I'm no worse off than I was two weeks ago. Unfortunately I'm no better off, either. I really thought I was making progress last week, what with Svetlana and Cyndi-O, and then—" Her optimistic facade crumbled. "Oh, Jay, it's been a really crummy morning!"

She proceeded to tell him, in horrific detail, every rotten phone call and visitor she'd had that day. She feared that he would overreact when she told him about David's resignation. She thought he might insist on jumping in and taking over her photo studio; instead he made only a mild offer that if she got in a bind he could probably squeeze an extra job into his schedule. His restraint amazed and delighted her.

Jay was so gently supportive, so nonjudgmental, that Halley unloaded on him as she'd seldom done before. When she realized she'd been bending his ear for almost twenty minutes, she finally stopped herself. "Good heavens, why didn't you shut me up?" she asked. "You must have better things to do than listen to me moan and groan."

"Not a thing in the world," he assured her. "And you feel better, don't you?"

"No. Well, yes, I suppose so." Actually she did. She'd had no idea that simply unloading on a sympathetic listener would be so therapeutic. "Only one thing would make me feel better."

"Oh? And what's that?" There was definitely a seductive bent to his question.

"Several thousand dollars in tens and twenties would be nice," she quipped.

"That *would* be pleasant," Jay agreed with an indulgent chuckle. "Listen, I'll make dinner tonight, okay? You just come home and relax."

"That's a deal."

After Jay had hung up, Halley left the phone off the hook for just a minute or two longer. She really did feel better.

Jay's emotional support was like a soothing balm to her frazzled nerves. She was beginning to realize that she had overlooked a tremendous source of comfort and inspiration in Jay. There was no reason for her to fear his moral support would become some kind of crutch. She could easily get used to it, true, but if he suddenly withdrew it, life would go on.

Then again, if she'd tried to confide in Jay like this a few months or years ago, his reaction would have been different, she was sure. She could almost hear his voice in her head—advising, second-guessing, trying to fix everything for her.

That well-meaning interference of his was an ingrained tendency, not something he could eliminate overnight. He must be trying awfully hard, she thought with a fond smile. Good for him. Good for both of them.

With reluctance she hung up her phone, then buzzed Kathryn to get her messages. Time to face the lions again.

The afternoon crept by at an agonizingly slow pace, until another diversion appeared at a little after three o'clock. As Halley talked with the Korman Building landlord over the phone, one of the secretaries brought a package back to Halley's office, slipping in quietly and dropping it into the In basket.

Halley was trying to reassure Frank Bonner that she wouldn't be skipping out on her lease. As she talked, she glanced at the bulky manila envelope, noting the words Personal and Confidential. The name of the sender was conspicuously absent.

Trouble, she thought. Anonymous packages always were.

"The first of the month isn't until Wednesday," she said patiently into the phone. "Let's not borrow trouble, Frank. If for some reason I can't pay you in a timely manner, we can discuss it then, all right?"

After finally managing to dislodge him from the phone, she hung up and turned her full attention to the package. "Might as well get it over with," she mumbled as she used her brass letter opener to work her way through the thick packing tape. Then she peeked inside—and almost fainted. What the...?

With clumsy hands she turned the package upside-down and dumped the contents onto her desk blotter. The crisp green bills fluttered into a sizable pile. Not tens and twenties, but fifties and hundreds.

Her phone buzzed as she counted them. She ignored it. She had to know how much was here. When she was done with her tally, she could hardly believe it. The envelope had contained just under eight thousand dollars.

"Halley, why didn't you answer your—omigod!" Kathryn skidded to a stop in the doorway. "Where did that come from?"

"From the package that just arrived. By messenger service?"

Kathryn nodded, turning pale.

"Which one?"

"I, um, don't remember. Just a guy in a khaki uniform with a clipboard. I can call the doorman. He might have noticed."

"No, don't bother. I know where it came from." She scooped up the piles of money and stuffed them back into the envelope.

"How...how much is there?" Kathryn asked in a whisper.

"Enough to pay our rent, the phone bill, and the IRS, with some left over," Halley replied. "Unfortunately we can't spend a dime of it."

"I won't even ask."

"Wise choice. Kathryn, would you hold my calls for, oh, about ten minutes?"

"Sure," Kathryn replied. Seeming to sense Halley's need for solitude, she backed out the door and closed it without another word.

The moment she was alone Halley dialed Jay's number for the second time that day. She took several deep breaths and consciously unclenched her fists as she waited for an answer.

This time Peg picked up the phone. Halley quickly learned that Jay had already gone home for the day. Deflated, she hung up.

If only she hadn't voiced aloud her wish for cold hard cash. Obviously she'd presented a temptation too great for Jay to resist. *Why couldn't he leave well enough alone?* she railed silently, looking wistfully at the roses.

Jay hummed tunelessly as he prepared two heavenly pork chops for the broiler. A little rosemary, a little tarragon—he knew nothing about spices, so he just sniffed the various bottles and sprinkled on whatever smelled good. He'd already grated cheese and chopped chives for the two fat potatoes baking in the oven. The broccoli was cut up and ready for the vegetable steamer. A bottle of white wine was chilling in the fridge.

He wasn't a terribly skilled cook. He could handle the basics when the need arose, but it seemed to take him forever. He'd left the studio at three o'clock just so he'd have enough time to shop and make all necessary preparations for the early dinner he had planned.

He was anxious for Halley to get home. He wanted to treat her to good food, good wine, and scintillating conversation guaranteed to take her mind off her troubles. Then, after a leisurely meal, they would retire to the living room and watch the Tracy/Hepburn video he'd rented. Mindless comedy—that's what she liked to watch when she'd had a bad day. This one would put her in a suitably relaxed mood for...well, for whatever. He wouldn't push, but he couldn't help hoping.

The front door banged open at five-thirty, and an icy breeze brought Halley inside. Jay greeted her with a properly chaste kiss on the cheek. She glared at him, her eyes colder than the wind. He tried to help her off with her coat. She batted his hands away.

"Stop fussing over me," she groused, pulling off the coat by herself.

"I take it your afternoon wasn't any better than your morning," he observed dryly.

"Oh, I don't know." She strode through the living room, then slammed her briefcase down on the breakfast bar. "I wouldn't call an unexpected windfall of eight thousand dollars bad, now, would you?"

He didn't like the dangerous edge to her voice—not at all. Someone had made her awfully angry, and whoever it was had better watch his or her back. He decided to try a gentle approach one more time. "Do you want to tell me what happened?"

She whirled around to face him, reminding him of nothing so much as a cat with her back up. A mean cat, he amended. "Are you going to stand there and pretend you don't know?" she demanded.

He stared at her for several seconds, blinking in surprise. "Halley, what are you talking about?" His words were edged with impatience. If she believed he'd committed some heinous crime, she'd better come out and accuse him of it. He refused to play mouse to her cat.

She turned back to the briefcase, flipped up the latches with quick, efficient movements, and opened it. She pulled out a yellow envelope and slapped it down on the counter. "I suppose you've never seen this before."

"I don't know. What is it?"

"Take a look for yourself," she answered, sounding not quite as sure of herself.

He did, and what he saw inside shocked him speechless. He reached inside the envelope and pulled out handful after handful of money. "How much is here?" he asked when he'd found his voice.

"Seven thousand, nine hundred and fifty dollars, to be exact. It was bad enough you paid off my credit card. But there is no way I can accept—"

"You think I'm responsible for this?" he interrupted.

"Well, aren't you?"

"Are you crazy? What makes you think I have this kind of money lying around?"

"I just assumed you did. You paid that three-thousand-dollar Visa bill without blinking an eye."

"And that pretty much wiped me out. Besides, even if I did have that kind of pocket change, I wouldn't be stupid enough to just send it to you. We agreed, I wouldn't interfere that way anymore."

"And I agreed to ask if I needed your help. I thought maybe you interpreted that phone call I made today as asking for help."

"No. I expect you'd be a bit more direct."

Wordlessly Halley stuffed the money back in its container and thrust it into her briefcase. "Well, what was I supposed to think?" she asked defensively when he continued to stare at her in stony silence. "I make an offhand wish for several thousand dollars, and poof, two hours later several thousand dollars drop into my lap. Unless my phone is tapped, you're the only one who heard me make that wish. And you're the only one who would give me money."

"Obviously you're mistaken." He couldn't help feeling a little self-righteous. Anyone would, being accused so unjustly.

"What's for dinner?" she asked.

"You're changing the subject."

"If you didn't send the money, what more is there to talk about?"

"Do you believe me?"

She hesitated a moment. "Yes. I trust you."

It was a less-than-enthusiastic vote of confidence, but he decided to let it slide. "In that case, we're having pork chops for dinner," he said, softening a bit. "Are you hungry?"

"Truthfully, my stomach's a little upset. Do we have any milk?"

"I'll get you some," he offered, attempting to slide by her and into the kitchen.

She grabbed his hand and pulled him back, a rueful look on her face. Then she put her arms around his neck and hugged him, bringing her soft, desirable body into dangerous contact with his. "I'm sorry, Jay," she whispered in his ear. "I had no right to accuse you like that."

As he held her close, the rest of his anger dissolved. He could forgive her just about anything when she was in his arms. He wondered if she knew that. "It's been a long, hard day," he said. "I guess I shouldn't blame you for thinking I sent that money, under the circumstances. Hell, it even sounds like something I'd do."

He brushed her lips, quickly, with his. He couldn't resist; she was so conveniently close. She started to pull away, then stopped. Her eyes seemed to darken as she gazed at him uncertainly.

He wanted her. Of course, lately that was a perpetual state for him, and he fought a constant battle holding back. But that shadow of doubt and vulnerability he sensed in her tested his willpower.

"Even if you did do it," she said slowly, "it was an extraordinarily generous gesture, if a misguided one. I shouldn't have gotten so angry."

"But I didn't do it." He tried to read her mind by staring into her eyes. "You don't really believe me, do you?" He ought to be insulted. Instead he felt tolerant, benevolent, and unreasonably affectionate.

"I want to believe you, and I do, really..." Her voice trailed off.

He sighed. "Oh, ye of little faith. I just might have slipped you some anonymous cash, if I'd thought of it first. But I would have found a less obvious way to give it to you."

"How would you do it?" she asked, her arms still looped around his neck. "I'm curious."

"Well, let's see." He thought for a moment. "I'd arrange to have the money come through one of your 'bad debt' accounts receivable—like that magazine that owed you so much money and then declared bankruptcy. You would never suspect it. But haven't we talked enough about money for one night?"

He leaned down to kiss her again, attempting to re-establish the intimate mood. But just as their lips almost touched, the oven timer sounded with an intrusive buzz.

"Dinner?" she asked breathlessly.

He kissed her on the nose, instead of his original target. "Dinner," he confirmed, knowing the disappointment showed on his face. "I'll get you that milk."

"No, never mind. My stomach feels better now." She released him. "Do I have time to change clothes?"

At his nod she retreated to her bedroom. Close call, she thought as she shut the door behind her.

She rifled through her closet for a comfortable alternative to her itchy suit, half-aware that something odd had happened to her thinking processes back there. She'd been so furious only minutes earlier, and now she couldn't muster any anger at all—despite the fact that she still wasn't sure about Jay's innocence.

If he did send her the cash, he did it because he cared for her. Maybe it was that realization that had doused the fire of her anger so quickly, kindling a dangerous desire in its place.

Giving in to that desire wasn't a good idea, she reminded herself. At this point, sex would only muddy the waters, fooling them into a false sense of harmony that was a long way away. They still had a lot of work to do, a lot of repairs to make to their battered relationship.

She removed the suit and hung it up, still at a loss as to what to put on. A sweatsuit would be the safest thing, given the electric charge that had passed between herself and Jay only moments ago. Nice, baggy, unflattering sweats. But she couldn't find any, and at the last minute she reached for a caftan made of violet and gold batiste. It covered her from her neck to her wrists and toes. What could be safer?

By the time she returned, Jay had served their dinner. Two tall candles bathed the linen-covered table in a soft glow. He'd used their wedding china, linen napkins, and . . . plastic tumblers for water glasses. The good crystal was packed in one of her boxes stacked in the living room, she remembered with a twinge.

"This looks so elegant," she said.

"So do you. I've always liked that purple thing you're wearing."

She didn't know what to reply, so she took her seat without saying anything, wishing belatedly she'd persevered until she'd found the sweatsuit.

A highly charged silence kept them company through most of dinner. Jay studied Halley, wondering what happened to that scintillating conversation he'd planned. He couldn't think of anything to talk about. His mind was filled to the brim with images of her. The thin purple cloth of her caftan whispered whenever she moved, shifting across her delicate shoulders, draping along her slender arms, shaping and reshaping itself over her breasts. If she'd chosen her apparel deliberately to drive him crazy, it was working.

"There's ice cream for dessert, if you'd like," he said a few minutes later, after Halley had set her napkin on the table with a satisfied sigh. "I could make some coffee."

"Thank you, but no; I couldn't eat or drink another mouthful. Everything was delicious." She scooted her chair back and reached for her plate, as if to carry it to the kitchen, but he stopped her.

"Let me do that," he offered. "I intended for you to take the whole night off. Stretch out on the sofa and put your feet up. I'll join you shortly and we can watch the movie I rented."

She gave him a grateful smile before following his advice.

Jay made short work of the dishes as his body thrummed with anticipation. Even if they didn't end up in bed, he looked forward to spending a relaxed, undemanding evening with Halley. She needed the time off. And more importantly, the two of them needed some down time together, to confirm that they still could enjoy each other outside the bedroom. That seemed important, at this stage of the game.

When the kitchen was straightened up and the dishwasher running, Jay strode purposefully into the living room. He found the TV on and Halley sprawled languorously on the couch, just as he'd planned. Then he saw the remote control on the floor, where it had fallen out of her limp hand. She was fast asleep.

Disappointment sliced through him. It was all he could do to resist waking her up. But the stress of the last couple of weeks had taken its toll on her, and right now she probably needed a good night's sleep a lot more than she needed his attentions. With a sigh he scooped her up. She didn't stir. He started to carry her into the guest room, then realized he'd have to unfold the sofa bed before he could put her down for the night.

"Forget that," he murmured, carrying her into his bedroom instead. There would be hell to pay when she woke up and found herself there beside him, but at the moment he didn't care.

Eight

Halley awoke to the pleasant sensation of Jay nibbling on her neck. She lay on her side with her back against his chest, his arm around her, his hand resting negligently on her breast and his hard arousal pressed unmistakably into the small of her back.

"Jay?" she said softly, so as not to disturb the mood, "what am I doing here?"

Obviously he was still too sleepy to comprehend or answer, because he continued his inquisitive nibbles without a pause.

It didn't matter, she thought, shivering with undeniable pleasure. She had a pretty good idea what had happened last night. She'd accidentally fallen asleep, and he'd carried her into his room rather than wrestle with the stupid hide-a-bed in the guest room.

He had assumed a bit much, but she could hardly claim he'd taken advantage of her, seeing as she was still fully clothed in the modest caftan. She ought to be pleased that he hadn't left her on the couch, where she probably would have awakened with a kink in her neck.

She gloried in the sensations of his caresses another minute or two before taking action. Tempting though it was to blank her mind and remain just where she was, enjoying Jay's attentions, the clock said it was after seven. She should have been up and dressed long before now.

Resolutely she covered his roving hand with hers and gently pulled it away from her body so she could sit up. He gave a low groan of protest.

"Come back here," he said, still drowsy sounding.

"No, no, Jay," she cajoled, smiling despite herself at the replay of this familiar morning battle. "It's time to get up. We've overslept." She scooted off the bed and skittered away from him before he could grab her and launch a persuasive campaign that could easily make her forget about other obligations.

She watched from the doorway as he rubbed his face and sat up. When she was sure he was really awake, she left him and went to the kitchen to start the coffee.

Usually she managed to beat him to the shower, but this time she was too slow. So she laid out her clothes and accessories for the day, poured herself half a cup of coffee, then stood by the bathroom door and waited as she sipped the strong brew.

She didn't have to wait long. Moments later he emerged from the steam-filled room wearing nothing but a towel. Water droplets clung to the curly blond hair on his chest, and Halley felt a ridiculous urge to take his towel and blot him dry.

"Oh, hi," he greeted her, seeming taken aback at finding her there. "Sleep well?" He graced her with his most winning smile, then waited—to see what kind of mood she was in, she imagined.

She could have made life difficult for him. She could have given him all kinds of grief for taking her into his bed without her consent. But he looked so hopeful—not to mention sexy—she didn't have the heart.

"I slept for almost twelve uninterrupted hours," she replied. "And you?"

"Not great," he admitted.

She raised one skeptical eyebrow. "Conscience bothering you?"

At least he had the good grace to look chagrined. "No, it was more like hormones bothering me."

Damn, he looked attractive when he was squeaky clean and half-naked. Such an observation was not helpful at the moment, and Halley tried to suppress it, but there it was. Her own hormones were hardly comatose, and she became suddenly aware of her own rumpled, gritty-feeling body.

"You mad?" he asked when she said nothing.

She laughed, unable to continue the farce. "No. What else do you do with a woman who has the bad manners to fall asleep after such a lovely dinner, except put her in bed?" She handed him her empty cup. "Coffee's ready. Could you make some orange juice?"

He nodded, seemingly a bit dazed by her ready forgiveness. She ought to be more tolerant on a regular basis, she decided as she slipped into the bathroom. Too frequently she blew small things out of proportion, and Jay was often as not the unfortunate victim of her temper.

When she entered the kitchen a few minutes later, she found Jay talking on the phone.

"Here she is now," he said to the caller, then held the receiver out to Halley. "It's your mother."

Halley cringed inwardly with guilt as she took the phone, though she managed a cheerful greeting. She had talked to her mother only briefly when she'd returned from Europe and had promised to call within the week for a lengthy chat. She'd forgotten.

"I hope you don't mind me calling so early, honey," Cora Hays said, "but I wanted to do it before the rates go back up. You know how your father is about the long-distance bill."

Yes, she certainly did. "It's fine, Mom," she said. "Why don't you let me call you back at lunchtime and we can talk on my dime?"

"Oh, heavens, no," Cora replied, sounding horrified. "From the looks of things you can ill afford to be extravagant."

"So, you heard."

Jay refilled her coffee cup and set it on the counter in front of her. She mouthed a "thank you" to him.

"Your cousin Marsha read about you in the newspaper and phoned me," Cora said grimly. "Honey, why didn't you call and tell us?"

"I didn't want to bother you," Halley answered uneasily. "It's my problem, after all."

"But we want to be bothered. Your father is absolutely beside himself with worry, not to mention a little miffed because you didn't confide in us. He's ready to jump in the car and come to New York—"

"He wouldn't, would he?" Halley broke in, utterly panicked. The thought of trying to deal with her father on top of everything else literally made her stomach turn. His brand of interference made Jay look like a rank amateur.

"No, no, I convinced him not to fly off the handle. But, sweetheart, if you need money, your father can help."

Halley recoiled inwardly at the very thought. "I can do without that kind of help."

"I don't know what you mean."

"You of all people should know exactly what I'm talking about. Sure, Dad would love to help me out—as long as it doesn't inconvenience him. Then, the moment it does, *wham!* He'd pull the plug on me." Halley noticed that Jay was watching her intently. "I won't even consider it," she finished.

"You really think your father's that cold-blooded?" Cora asked, her voice faint.

"Not cold-blooded, just selfish and manipulative," Halley clarified, feeling not the slightest bit guilty. She loved her father, but she recognized his faults, too.

"You were only a child then," Cora said. They both knew what "then" meant. "You don't really understand what happened."

"I was sixteen. I saw and heard enough to know that he pulled the rug out from under you. He took away your dream."

There was a long pause. "My dream was to marry and raise a family," she said firmly.

Loyal to the end, Halley thought. Perhaps her mother was right—she never would understand.

"Why don't you come home for a visit?" Cora added impulsively. "Maybe you could just talk to your father."

"I'd like to visit, but . . ." Halley automatically thought of a dozen reasons why she couldn't get away. "Maybe in a couple of weeks. But I won't change my mind about Dad. Besides, I'm doing fine, really. Bouncing back. I don't need any help."

Cora sighed. "Fine, dear, if you say so. Just one more thing. If you and Jay are divorced, why does he answer your phone?" she asked with deceptive innocence.

"It's a long story," Halley answered. "I'll tell you about it sometime."

"All right," Cora replied with a little chuckle. "You don't have to tell me at all if you don't want to. Give him my love. I still love him even if he's not my son-in-law anymore."

"I'll tell him." Halley glanced at her watch as they concluded the call. She was really late.

"What was that all about?" Jay asked.

"Mom gives you her love," she answered. She took one final sip of her coffee before dumping the rest down the drain and setting her cup in the sink.

"No, I mean the other stuff, about your dad," he said, blocking her exit from the kitchen.

She waved her hand in a dismissive gesture. "Oh, that's just old family stuff. It's not important."

"I think it is." He had a curious light in his eyes.

She looked at her watch again. "Jay, I'm late for work." The phone rang. She answered it impatiently, not surprised to find Kathryn on the other end of the line.

"Where are you?" Kathryn asked.

"Running late," Halley answered, giving Jay a meaningful look. "Is there a problem?"

"Just wanted you to know that the guy from Cyndi-O wants to talk to you. I told him you would call him."

"Joe Spangler? Oh, I'd better get in touch with him right away." Maybe that door wasn't closed after all, she thought with a ray of hope. "Anything else?"

Jay listened for a moment, realizing that Halley's business would have to take precedence over his curiosity. He left her to make her phone calls in private. But he couldn't forget the one-sided conversation he'd overheard between her and her mother. Something about it had piqued his curiosity. He was almost sure that whatever they'd talked about had some bearing on his present situation with Halley. He intended to find out what it was, even if he had to call Cora and ask her.

Halley sat at her desk and pondered her latest work-related dilemma. The Cyndi-O account was still a possibility, but her most recent conversation with the designer, Joe

Spangler, left her in a quandary. Several weeks ago Joe had seen her chatting with Maureen Argent at a party and had mistakenly come to the conclusion that the Mystique Agency represented Maureen. Now he'd gotten it into his head that he wanted Maureen to be one of Cyndi-O's runway models for a series of upcoming shows.

Halley knew she should have spoken up right away, but she hadn't. Instead—without ever really lying—she'd told Joe that she would talk to Maureen.

Halley wondered if she hadn't been too rigid where Maureen was concerned. The woman was still a money-maker, despite her slightly off-color reputation. And if she had Maureen in her pocket, she stood a much better chance of enticing Joe to sign a contract. Impulsively she pulled Maureen's card out of her file and dialed the number.

Maureen answered with a groggy sounding "H'lo?" despite the late hour.

Halley promised herself not to make any rash decisions. She'd just feel Maureen out, explore a few possibilities. "It's Halley," she said with a forced smile in her voice. "I know it's last-minute, but are you free for lunch today?"

"For you, darling, of course," Maureen replied, immediately perking up. "Just name the time and place."

After the arrangements were made and Halley had hung up, she felt very uncomfortable about the whole thing. A few weeks ago she never would have considered taking on Maureen. "Desperate times call for desperate measures," she murmured.

A couple of hours later, as she was on the way out the door for the lunch appointment, Kathryn stopped her for a phone call. "It's Ms. Winsome, from the bank," she announced.

Great, just what she needed. Halley stepped into an empty side office to talk with Ms. Winsome, who was anything but what her name implied. After a stiffly worded, five-minute conversation, Halley reentered the foyer, feeling as if every drop of her blood had drained to her feet.

"Is it bad?" Kathryn asked.

"The bank's going to call in our loan," she said in a monotone. "If we aren't current by five o'clock today, that's it."

"But we can't make it," Kathryn objected, sounding as panicky as Halley felt.

"See what you can do with collections," she said, trying hard to reflect confidence. "Get one of the secretaries or booking agents to help you. I have to make this lunch appointment, but I'll think of something as soon as I get back."

She thought wistfully of the eight thousand untouchable dollars she'd stashed in a separate savings account this morning. She would use it only as a last resort, she promised herself as she stepped out into the crisp winter day. She wouldn't dip into Jay's money unless there was no other way. Even then, she wasn't sure. What if Jay wasn't responsible? What if, she thought with sudden insight, her father had sent her that money?

Maureen was her usual catty self as they settled down to a hurried lunch of fettuccine Alfredo. She'd read Cecily's column—with great relish, Halley imagined—and clucked with pseudosympathy for five minutes straight.

Though it galled her, Halley launched into the reason she'd arranged this lunch in the first place. "Maureen, I've been thinking about things, and I've decided that it might be a good idea after all for the Mystique Agency to represent you." She paused, waiting for a reaction.

Maureen studied her calmly as she pulled a cigarette from a gold case and lit it with a flourish. "But I thought my *style* wasn't *compatible* with yours," she objected, subconsciously touching her hat—a hat that would have looked ludicrous even on Princess Diana.

Halley hurried on, hating the position she was in. "I've painted myself into a corner by keeping my sights so narrow. The agency needs more diversity."

Maureen peered at her speculatively. "Are things that bad?"

"What—what do you mean?" Halley stuttered.

"Two weeks ago you wouldn't touch me with the proverbial ten-foot pole. You must be desperate."

Halley took a long sip from her wine glass. She'd lost the upper hand here. Time to fish or cut bait. "Do you want me to represent you or not?" she asked flatly.

"Not," Maureen answered with a vindictive smile. "Not until I'm satisfied that you're financially sound, anyway. Talk to me in a month or so."

In your dreams, Halley thought. She must have been crazy to even consider this. She was actually relieved Maureen had turned her down.

Maureen took a long puff of her cigarette. "Say, you haven't changed your mind about the fur, too, have you?"

The ultimate put-down, Halley thought, fuming inwardly while keeping a calm outward demeanor. Then again, it was just the break she needed. She steeled herself for what had to be done. "Five thousand dollars. Cash. If you can pull it together before three o'clock, the coat's yours."

Maureen smiled triumphantly. "My bank's just around the corner."

By the time Halley returned to the office she was shivering from the cold, but she had five thousand dollars in her purse. Without a word she fanned the cash out on the reception desk.

Kathryn looked up, her green eyes as round as Little Orphan Annie's. "Where did *that* come from?"

"Call Ms. Winsome," Halley instructed without answering the question. "Tell her I'm on my way to see her, to bring our account up to date. Oh, and, can I borrow your coat?''

Kathryn gasped. "You hocked your fox!"

Halley nodded glumly. "I was tired of the ratty old thing anyway."

It was almost eleven p.m., and Jay wasn't home yet. As Halley sat curled in an easy chair in the living room, leafing through a stack of trade magazines, she felt lonely, dejected, and unreasonably abandoned.

Tonight of all nights she'd looked forward to Jay's comforting presence. She'd wanted his wide shoulders to lean on, his strong arms curved protectively around her. She had quickly grown accustomed to having Jay there for her, and that scared her a little.

It wasn't just the fact that she'd come to rely on him, to need him. That was scary enough. But what really shook her was the way Jay seemed to thrive on nurturing her.

Her financial catastrophe had brought them closer, fostering a new degree of understanding between them. All that was fine and good, for now. But what about later? What about after she'd bounced back from this disaster, and was once again standing on her own two feet, strong and independent? She had no doubts that she *would* recover, in time. Her real concerns centered on how Jay would react to that.

Though she would always need him in her life, the nature of her needs wouldn't continue to be as dramatic as they were now. Eventually she wouldn't have to lean on his financial resources, his material support. Would emotional support be enough for Jay to give? Or was her current, needy state part of what attracted him to her?

Her mind wandered to the anonymous cash she'd received yesterday. If Jay was responsible, it seemed a pretty strong indication that he wanted to give Halley more than she was willing to take. She fervently hoped she was wrong, that he hadn't sent that money. But if he didn't, who did?

All these questions were daunting, but time would eventually reveal the answers. She'd already learned many surprising things during the past weeks. Today, for instance, she had learned that she could swallow her pride and survive a dose of humility without curling up and dying. Accepting help—even Maureen's patronizing brand—was unpleasant but survivable, and knowing that was a victory of sorts.

Halley was overcome with relief when she heard Jay's keys rattling in the door. Today had been the pits, and she so looked forward to his soothing words. If she were honest, she'd admit that she looked forward to more than words. She wanted to make love, to share the ultimate act that for Halley confirmed the basic goodness of life.

When Jay came through the door, however, she was forced to alter her plans. One look at his face told her that something was definitely amiss. She could almost see thunderclouds hanging over his head.

She rose from her chair to greet him. "What's wrong?" she asked immediately.

His gaze softened when it fell on her. "Hi. Guess I'm a little late for dinner. I should have called."

"You didn't miss much," she confessed. "Just a casserole. Want me to warm it up?"

He nodded. "That would be great."

As she prepared a plate for the microwave, she tried to fight her own disappointment. This was no time to seek comfort from Jay, she realized. He obviously had his own problems. She felt suddenly selfish. All this time she and Jay had been focusing solely on her dilemma; it had never occurred to her that he might have troubles of his own.

Whatever was wrong, she'd help him get through it, she vowed as she set the microwave timer. When it was humming, she turned away from it to find Jay sitting at the breakfast bar, his chin resting in his hand. He was staring off into space. She'd never seen him look so world weary.

Without asking she pulled a bottle of beer from the fridge, twisted off the cap, and set it in front of him. "Here, you look like you could use this."

He gave her a halfhearted smile of appreciation. "Thanks, but I need something else a whole lot more."

"And what's that?" she asked, her heart pounding.

"You."

In the batting of an eyelash she was next to him. He swiveled around on the barstool to face her, pulling her between his thighs. Her arms went around his neck. His welcoming lips were warm, soft, languorous, though not urgent. It was the kind of embrace that could be enjoyed for itself—not necessarily a prelude to lovemaking.

The kiss ended by mutual consent, though they continued to hold each other. Halley stroked his firmly muscled back in a soothing rhythm. "Are you going to tell me what's wrong?" she asked.

"I was getting to it. My studio was burglarized."

"Oh, no," Halley said on a sigh.

"In broad daylight, no less. Peg was out on a shoot, and I left the warehouse for maybe thirty minutes, to get a haircut and grab lunch. I locked the door, but I didn't set the alarm," he admitted.

"What did they take?" she asked, pressing her cheek against his hair as she rubbed the tense muscles of his neck.

"Everything that wasn't nailed down. They had a panel truck. They broke a window, then proceeded to carry everything right out the front door. I saw them leaving when I came back."

"I guess nothing's really safe," she said.

"Nothing," he agreed solemnly. "I've spent all afternoon and evening dealing with the police and the insurance company. I finally tracked Peg down a couple of hours ago. She keeps an itemized list of our equipment, with serial numbers, and we needed that for the police report."

"Is there any hope you'll catch whoever did it?" Halley asked, already suspecting the answer.

"Not much. I had a good description of the truck, and a sketchy description of the guy driving, but I didn't notice the license number."

"Insurance will cover it all, though, right?"

He nodded. "But it'll take awhile to get it settled. Meantime, I'm dead in the water."

"Oh, Jay," she said, feeling helpless. "Is there anything I can do?"

"Just hold me," he said, wrapping his arms more tightly around her.

That she could do, and more. She pushed his hair away from his forehead and pressed her lips against his brow, trying to kiss away the furrows there.

Jay closed his eyes and let Halley's warm mouth wander over him. What a wonderful thing to come home to, he thought, allowing some of the nervous tension to leave his body. Immediately he acknowledged another kind of tension, a much more pleasant sort, as Halley teased his ear with her tongue.

Her restless hands ruffled his hair and caressed the skin beneath the collar of his yellow cotton shirt. When she slid them between their bodies and began toying with the hem of his sweater, he realized her intent.

"Wait a minute," he said.

"Mmm, what's wrong?" she asked in a sultry voice, pulling the sweater over his head despite his protest.

"I'm not a charity case, am I?"

She laughed, a deep throaty sound. "What?"

"I seem to recall you saying we shouldn't make this sort of thing a habit. You're not doing this because you feel sorry for me, are you?"

"No, Jay," she reassured him as she began to unfasten his buttons. "I've been planning just how I would do this since I came home this afternoon. Anyway, twice isn't a habit."

He pulled back enough that he could look into her eyes. The desire he saw there stilled his doubts. He ran his fingertip down the front of her prim-and-proper white blouse, all the way to the waist of her slim black skirt. "You don't look as though you dressed with seduction in mind," he commented lazily.

"Wanna make a bet?" She stepped back and slowly untied the bow at her neck. Jay sucked in his breath as her nimble fingers worked the long row of buttons down the front of her blouse, allowing him a provocative glimpse of something shiny underneath. She undid her cuff links with deliberate languor, then pulled the blouse free of the skirt.

Jay made an involuntary sound of surprise and admiration as the blouse slid to the floor, revealing her peach silk camisole. Her skin glowed with a life all its own—golden on her shoulders, creamier where the tops of her small, perfect breasts peeked out from behind the lace-edged undergarment.

He took a sip of his beer to ease the dryness in his throat as he urged her with his eyes to continue the impromptu striptease. Her black skirt soon joined the blouse on the floor, and she was left standing before him in the raciest lingerie he'd ever seen her wear. The camisole was complemented by string bikini bottoms, sheer stockings, and a cream lace garter belt.

He decided, right then, that whoever had invented panty hose should be shot.

She pulled the pins out of her neat hairstyle and shook her head, so that the glorious, dark sable waves cascaded over her shoulders. Some women might be self-conscious, standing before a man in such an outfit. Not Halley. She was obviously proud of her body. She stood unflinching before him, chin up, shoulders back, breasts thrust forward, as he made a visual examination of her from head to toe.

"Well?" she said when his eyes returned to hers. "Would you like to retire?" She held out a hand as if to lead him to the bedroom.

He took her hand and surprised her by kissing it. "You look much too exotic to hide away in a bedroom. I want you here, now. On the rug in front of the fireplace."

"That's not a fireplace, it's a wood stove," she objected, though by the way she smiled, he could tell she liked the idea.

"Use your imagination, Halley," he said as he quickly shrugged out of his shirt.

"I'm already using it," she said in a deliberately suggestive voice. "Don't go away, I'll be right back." She left the room, her slim hips swaying seductively. She'd gone to get the condoms, he realized when she returned a moment later with something in her hand. It was a good thing she didn't depend on him to remember, he mused guiltily.

She went to the sofa and gathered up several throw pillows, which she tossed onto the rug in front of the stove as he watched, almost mesmerized by her simplest movement.

He wanted to kiss her again, to feel her quivering, heated skin beneath him. That urge warred with the one to get rid of the rest of his own uncomfortable clothes. Quickly he kicked his shoes off, unbuckled his belt, and shed denim and cotton with record speed.

He shut the light off before coming to her. He could still see her, illuminated by the fireglow. She stood waiting for him, and when he came closer her eyes contained a fire all their own, just for him.

"You are the most beautiful man," she murmured as she reached for him.

"Beautiful?" he questioned as he welcomed her sweetness close to him again. "That's hardly a word to describe a man." He kissed her neck where it met with the delicious slope of her shoulder.

"Beautiful, the same way a tiger is beautiful, or a stallion. Fast, powerful, a little dangerous..."

"You wax poetic, Hal." He wrapped both of his hands around her lace-covered breasts as he breathed in the soft scent of her hair.

"You don't like to hear me talk?" she teased gently. "You'd rather I lie quietly?"

"I love to hear you talk. I love you, period."

They both grew very still.

"God help me, I do, Halley," he said, sliding his hands around her and squeezing her until she thought she'd have to quit breathing. "I never *stopped* loving you. You're in my blood and you'll be there always, I'm afraid. Let me love you."

"Yes." It was all she needed to say. Her eyes filled with tears of some unnamed emotion as he eased her ever so gently to the pillows on the carpet. She wasn't sure if it was his brain or his hormones talking, but his declaration moved her deeply. He wasn't a man who said those words often, in or out of bed.

He unfastened one stocking and slid it down with delicious slowness, pausing to kiss each inch of her leg as he exposed it. He repeated the process with the other stocking, her garter belt, her panties.

Though she was tempted to close her eyes and lose herself in tactile sensations, she kept them open so she could watch Jay, the play of muscles in his strong back, the play of expressions on his face. The sight of his rigid arousal excited her as his hands played her body like a fine musical instrument, stroking, brushing softly, sometimes adagio, sometimes allegro.

He eased her camisole upward, revealing her breasts in the firelight. They ached for his touch, and Halley moaned as he lay down beside her and teased one swollen nipple with his tongue.

"Now," she said. "I don't want to wait."

"Not yet," he whispered back as he paused to pull the camisole over her head. "We have the whole night ahead of us."

"I won't last the whole night if you keep this up," she scolded just before he claimed her lips with his. I'll pass out, she thought to herself. He kissed her long and hard until she was sure the floor was spinning beneath her. His hand wandered to the soft place between her legs and began a slow, exploratory massage.

It didn't take her long to reach the brink of ultimate pleasure. Jay seemed to sense it and pulled back. "Not yet," he said again with maddening finality.

"I beg to differ," she argued amiably. With a quick shift of her weight she pushed Jay onto his back, and suddenly it was she leaning over him. She swung one leg over his body and straddled him. She couldn't help but again compare him in her mind to a stallion. She was about to tame him, and it was high time, too. She smiled wickedly.

"It's physically impossible," he began, returning her smile, "for a woman to take a man without..." His voice trailed off when she lovingly grasped his firm maleness and guided him into her. As she slowly lowered herself onto him, he was at a distinct loss for words.

Once he was sheathed deeply inside her, she leaned forward and brushed her sensitive nipples against the curling hair on his chest. "You were saying?"

His smile had vanished. He tenderly brushed her hair away from her face. "You've got the reins, babe. I'm at your mercy, and I plan to enjoy every minute of it."

She began to move, slowly at first so she could savor all the different sensations, then faster as her confidence built. Words could scarcely describe the wonder she felt at the fire burning inside, glowing hotter and brighter with each passing moment, invading every cell of her body until she thought she might just disappear in a wisp of smoke. Her surroundings ceased to matter. The day, the time, her own name, were beyond her mental grasp. Only feelings remained—the physical feeling of Jay under her and inside her, the winds of desire rushing around her, and an overwhelming emotion trying to burst forth from her heart.

She wanted to tell him how she felt, but her mind was no longer capable of forming words. Her release came in a heated rush, like a dive from the highboard into a deep, warm pool of pure fulfillment.

Moments later she was only vaguely aware that Jay had followed her to that marvelous, mindless place she'd been. His breath came raggedly, and a thin sheen of perspiration covered his body. She leaned forward and lay against him, their bodies still joined. He kissed her brow and stroked her back in a way that made her feel precious.

They said nothing for a very long time, housed snugly in a sanctuary of silence. When at last Halley was able, she spoke the words she'd been unable to utter earlier. "I love you, too, Jay."

He pressed his lips against her hair. She could feel his warm breath against her scalp. "If I love you and you love me," he said, "explain to me again why we got divorced."

Nine

"Love was never the issue, you know that," Halley responded gently. "I think that's why it was so difficult. If we didn't care so much it wouldn't have hurt like it did."

"At the time I didn't think you felt anything," he said with a hint of the old resentment. "You were so distant."

"I guess I'm good at hiding things. It hurt, believe me. It still hurts."

There was another long silence. "Love by itself isn't enough, is it?" he asked.

"No, I guess it isn't," she managed to answer unemotionally, though his words were like a cold vise of fear squeezing her heart in two. Was he saying he didn't think they could make things work, after all? She was afraid to ask and so she didn't. As long as there was still hope, she could work toward a reconciliation, building on the progress they'd already made. She wouldn't give this up until he told her, point blank, that things were hopeless.

When the fire grew cold sometime later, they got to their feet and stumbled to the bedroom. They made love again, a slow, drowsy act that was nothing like their earlier, more frenzied joining. But it was rife with tenderness and sweet words, exciting in its own way yet reassuring, too.

As Halley was about to drift to sleep, an unromantic, totally incongruous thought struck her, and she wondered why it hadn't occurred to her before. Jay was without his photo equipment, and she was without a photographer. Now it made complete sense for him to move into the Mystique Agency studio, at least for a while.

She and Jay would be helping each other, a sort of mutual bailout. She could prove to Jay that she trusted him enough to involve him in her business, and if he behaved himself he just might prove to her that he was capable of intervening without taking over.

She'd spring her idea on him first thing in the morning.

Halley had to smile when she entered the living room the next morning and saw clothes and pillows scattered all over the floor. Jay's half-empty bottle of beer still sat on the breakfast bar, and she found the cold casserole in the microwave. Normally she hated waking up to a messy house, but this time she didn't mind. Tidying up hadn't been one of her priorities last night.

Since Jay had skipped dinner he was probably ravenous, she thought. In a generous mood, she decided to whip up a quick cheese omelet. It was early yet, so she was in no hurry to rush to the office.

She nearly flipped the omelet onto the ceiling when a pair of hands grasped her about the waist and warm lips pressed against her nape. "Jay!" she scolded.

"How did you know it was me?" he asked, trailing one finger down her arm as he moved toward the coffeepot.

"Lucky guess."

"You snuck out of bed before I was awake," he said, scowling at her with mock severity.

"I know. How else can I get to work on time?"

"Who's going to care if you're late?" he countered, studying her with more than casual interest. "You're the boss."

"I'd be setting a bad example for my employees... Jay, how many times have we had this discussion?"

"Oh, about every morning since you started the agency," he answered amiably.

"And how many times do you win?"

"About twenty percent of the time," he answered without hesitation.

"You've kept track?" she asked in a horrified voice.

He merely smiled enigmatically.

She sighed and shook her head. The man was incorrigible. "Get yourself a plate, I'll serve up this omelet."

"That's for me?" He seemed genuinely surprised.

"Of course it's for you. You know I don't eat breakfast."

"Is this a special occasion?" He set a place for himself at the bar, then refilled both of their coffee cups.

"Not exactly." She flipped the omelet onto his plate and set the pan in the sink. "I just thought you might be hungry, and, well, you had a bad day yesterday, and I wanted to get you off on the right foot this morning."

"Aha, just as I thought—I'm a charity case." But he softened the comment with a smile, then took an appreciative bite of the omelet.

"Speaking of yesterday," she said, settling onto the stool next to his, "I have an idea for how to make your life easier. Want to hear it?"

"Sure," he answered between bites, seemingly more interested in the eggs than what she had to say.

His attitude made her nervous about springing her idea on him, but she launched ahead. "How would you like to use my photo studio for a while?" she asked, all in a rush. "You and Peg. Just till you can get your own equipment replaced," she added when he made no response.

He looked at her uncertainly, with a tinge of some foreign emotion in his pale blue eyes. Irritation? Hurt? She couldn't read him, but the look made her squirm.

"You can even borrow some of my stuff and take it to your studio, if you'd feel more comfortable," she tried again.

Jay set his fork down and pushed the half-eaten omelet aside. "I don't think so, Halley. Thanks just the same."

"But Jay..." She stumbled. How could he so casually throw aside her wonderful idea without even thinking about it? What was she supposed to say in the face of such a bland dismissal?

"Look, Hal, I was sort of shook up when I came home last night," he said. "But everything is going to work out. I've got plenty of insurance, and I'll receive a check in a couple of days. It's no big deal."

"It *is* a big deal," she insisted. "Anyway, all my equipment is just sitting there since David left..."

"I'm not a charity case."

It was the third time he'd used that particular phrase, she realized, counting last night. "Why you arrogant, self-pitying—"

He looked up suddenly at her sharp tone.

"All I'm trying to do is help, and you—"

"I'm turning you down," he finished for her. "It just so happens I don't *need* your help."

She felt as if someone had heaved a football right into her midsection. In all the times she and Jay had argued, that had to be the most hurtful thing he'd ever said to her. She wanted to grab him by the shoulders, shake him, force him to take it back. But she didn't move. She just sat there, as the lump in the back of her throat grew larger and larger.

Jay sipped his coffee and stared off into space, apparently unaware of what he'd triggered.

As she tried without success to swallow the lump, another realization dawned on her. *I don't need your help.* How often had she said those exact words to Jay? A dozen times? A hundred? More than that, she'd bet. And she'd said them with never a second thought as to how they would make Jay feel. Selfishly, all she'd considered was her own foolish pride.

Her emotions did a swift turnabout. She wanted to kick herself good and hard for all the times she'd blithely hurt Jay without ever knowing. Now she understood—at least a little—how he felt when he saw her struggling and she staunchly, *stubbornly* refused to allow him to ease her burden.

Before she could stop it, an embarrassingly obvious sob slipped out.

Jay looked at her, his eyes wide with surprise. "Halley, you're crying!"

"No kidding."

"Why?" His immediate instinct was to reach for her, ready to comfort.

Her immediate instinct was to pull away, but this time she didn't. If he wanted her to cry on his shoulder, then by God she would. She flew to him and buried her face in his shirt. "I guess my emotions are running pretty close to the surface these days," she mumbled against his collarbone.

"It's okay," he soothed, rubbing her back. "I won't tell anyone I saw you crying."

She laughed and hiccuped all at the same time. "Oh, Jay, I just realized what a heartless wretch I've been."

"Oh?"

She took a deep breath. "When you turned down my idea, you made me feel just awful."

"I'm sorry," he said automatically. "I'll—"

"No, no, that's not the point," she said, cutting him off. "The point is, I must have made you feel just as awful, a million different times. I never realized—I just *never realized* how important it is to be able to help someone you love when they're in trouble, that's all."

"Oh, Halley." His voice was full of regret as he ran his fingers through her hair.

"The truth is, I'm the one who needs the help. I have a truckload of photo work to be done and no one to do it, and if I farm the work out to some other photographer, I'll lose a lot of money I can't afford to lose. I should have said that in the first place, instead of making it sound like I was doing you a big favor. I guess I wanted to feel like you needed my help, for a change."

He opened his mouth to object, stopped, and rested his chin on the top of her head to think.

"Do you see what I'm getting at?"

"Um, almost. Not quite." He slid off the barstool and, with his arm around Halley's shoulders, led her to the sofa. He sat down and settled her against him. "Are you saying you want me to use your photo equipment?"

She moved away from him so they could view each other eye to eye. "Listen to me, Jay, and listen good. I don't think I've ever told you this in so many words, but I need you."

"Then I'll start this afternoon," he said eagerly. "How much work do you actually have lined up?"

She gave him a pained expression. "Of course I need your photography skills, but I also need *you,* Jay."

He looked as if he still didn't quite understand.

"You've always been there for me, ready to help. I must seem ungrateful, because I so seldom *let* you help, but I knew you were there just the same, and I knew I could count on you. Even if your presence in my life is only tempo-rary—'' she paused to swallow as the lump reasserted itself "—please remember that I couldn't have gotten through this without you.''

He was smiling in a tender, wistful sort of way that made her heart twist beneath her breast.

"Am I just rambling wildly, or have I made my point?'' she asked.

In answer he pulled her roughly against him. "Halley, you don't really have to rush off to work, do you?''

"No, I have a few minutes,'' she said, thinking he might need to respond to the avalanche of words she'd just dumped on him.

"Good.'' He held her face pressed between his palms and kissed her with an almost desperate intensity. Her mind wanted to rebel, but her body responded in kind. It was amazing how quickly he could kindle desire in her. "How many minutes?'' he murmured against her lips.

"About ten, you despicable rogue,'' she answered, but she was already unfastening the buttons of her silk shirt-dress. At that moment she couldn't have denied him any-thing, particularly something she wanted just as badly as he did. "I pour my soul out and all you can think about is sex?'' She ought to be furious, she thought. She giggled.

His answer was suddenly serious. "The truth is I'm so touched I don't know what to say. I'd rather show you how I feel.''

"Now *that*,'' she said as she peeled off her dress, "is the best line I've ever heard.''

Exactly ten minutes later she was scurrying out the front door, smeared lipstick and all, but she wore a smile.

Jay invaded the Mystique Agency photo studio just after lunch. *Invaded* was perhaps too strong a word, and Halley scolded herself for thinking in those terms. She had to keep an open mind. But the aggressive yet meticulous way Jay approached his work was a far cry from David's more laid-back methods.

She spent almost an hour showing Jay how things were set up and explaining the work that needed to be done. Before he'd been there even five minutes, he started to rearrange things in the darkroom, almost unconsciously it seemed. She gritted her teeth and kept her mouth shut, reminding herself often that she had to let go a little.

The first few jobs she required of Jay were routine product shots. Or they *would* have been routine for David, who had done lots of jobs for this particular client. Jay, on the other hand, spent what seemed an inordinate amount of time getting the lights set up, taking light-meter readings, and fooling with Polaroid proofs.

Halley knew she should just leave him to it. She had plenty of work to keep her busy. But for some reason she felt compelled to stick around, to reassure herself that she'd communicated clearly the results she and the client expected.

When she made her umpteenth suggestion for improving the setup, Jay took a deep breath, walked away from the camera, then over to where Halley sat perched on a stool to oversee the work. He stood in front of her for a moment, clenching and flexing his hands, and she looked up at him warily. Finally he put his hands on her shoulders, gently but firmly.

"Don't you have something else to do?" he asked.

"You want me to leave." She knew she sounded resentful and wished she didn't.

"I can't work with you as a backseat driver," he stated flatly.

"But David always—"

"I'm not David," he reminded her. "Every photographer has his or her own methods, you know that. Maybe

I've been working for myself too long, but I have to do this my own way, okay?''

She nodded numbly. There was nothing for her to get upset about, she reminded herself. Surely she'd have the same proprietary feeling about this work with any new photographer, not just Jay. Still, his strong-willed, precise manner was hard to adjust to.

But adjust she would.

Jay didn't know it, but this was a test. If they could make this arrangement work and not kill each other in the process, it would prove, to Halley at least, that each of them had learned something over the past few weeks and that they were changing, or at least trying to change.

At the moment they were failing the test miserably. She felt resentful of his intrusion—even though she'd invited him here. For his part, he was aggressively taking over her studio. Without a word she hopped off the stool, breaking free of Jay's light grasp, and got out of there before she gave herself a chance to say or do something unbelievably stupid.

Jay watched her go with mixed feelings. This was the reason he'd declined her initial offer to let him use her equipment. He knew she'd have trouble letting go and allowing him to simply get the work done. To his credit, he'd taken her interference a lot longer than he would have a few weeks ago. To her credit, she'd exited before they could get into a real argument, and Halley usually was not one to back down from a fight.

He hoped she found a replacement photographer soon, because this arrangement would not last long. Meanwhile, he'd get through as many of these jobs as quickly as possible and squeeze in some of his own work, too. His goal here was to help them both out of a jam, not to impose his style of photography as the best or the only way it could be done.

The real trial would come on Friday, he thought, when two prospective models were coming in for some test shots. It was Halley's place to personally direct the photos, and that's when the differences between his style and David's would really come to light.

Over the next two days Halley stayed away from her own studio whenever Jay was there, though it drove her nearly crazy not to know what he was up to.

When one of the secretaries brought a purchase order from the studio for her approval, she hesitated before signing it. The supplies were essential, or Jay wouldn't have asked for them, she reasoned. But he was ordering a brand of products David had never used, and he was dealing with a vendor she'd never heard of. She picked up the phone, intending to question him about it, then stopped herself as the secretary watched her carefully.

This is not a big deal, she lectured herself. With her pen in a death grip, she scribbled her initials onto the form.

She nearly drove the rest of her staff crazy during what was left of the day. She insisted on knowing the status of every single model's bookings. She ordered a complete inventory of all office supplies. She went over the accounts with a Scrooge-like attitude, questioning every penny that came in or went out.

"What the hell's wrong with you?" Kathryn finally asked bluntly at the end of the second diabolical day. Halley had just finished raking her receptionist over the coals because she didn't think the message slips were filled out neatly enough. "I've been filling out your messages the same way for four years, and suddenly you don't like my *handwriting?*"

Halley sank into one of the foyer's red leather chairs, shaking her head. "Sorry, Kath. I'm just a little testy, I guess."

"A little? Have you noticed the way a room empties whenever you walk into it?"

"That bad?"

"Godzilla showed better interpersonal skills."

Halley chuckled. "At least I can count on you to be frank. You want a coffee before you head home? I'll buy. It's cold outside."

Kathryn looked at the rectangular clock on the wall. "It's still only quarter till five."

"Hang the switchboard," Halley said impulsively. "Let the answering service handle it. I want to buy you coffee."

"Okay," Kathryn agreed cheerfully. She made the necessary adjustments to the phone console, then went to the closet to retrieve Halley's coat and her own.

Halley took the hunter green wool coat, trying not to grimace. It was plain and conservative compared to the fox, but it was dignified.

"Don't you want to wait for Jay?" Kathryn asked as they started out the door. "I thought since he has a car today you'd hitch a ride home with him."

"No, I don't think that's a good idea," Halley answered, heading without hesitation to the elevators. "We need our space, as they say."

"Uh-oh. I thought you two were getting along."

"We were. Are." So far they'd avoided any serious arguments, she reflected with some satisfaction. They were treading carefully around one another at home, though, and she felt like one errant spark of temper could set them off like a shack full of dynamite.

"But it's stressful having him around, isn't it?" Kathryn asked.

"It's not simply his presence that's causing a problem," Halley elaborated, grateful for once to have a sympathetic ear. She needed to say some things aloud, just to clarify them in her own mind. "It's letting go of control of the studio that's about to kill me. I've been compensating by strengthening my hold on everything else, I guess."

"I'm glad to know you're acting compulsive for a reason," Kathryn quipped as they entered the crowded snack bar on the Korman Building's first floor.

Halley bought them both black coffee. She couldn't find an empty table, so they stood at a counter to drink it. "I know I've been awful today. I haven't driven anyone to the brink of resignation, have I?"

"No, but you do make everyone nervous. They start to wonder how bad things really are."

"I'm surprised more people haven't quit, like David."

"Only rats desert a sinking ship. Oops, I mean a *struggling* ship."

"It's a good thing you corrected yourself," Halley said with mock outrage. Abruptly she changed the subject. "I'm really nervous about those two girls coming in tomorrow."

"The Hankamer twins? Why? Halley, they're so photogenic a five-year-old with an Instamatic couldn't take a bad picture of those two."

How could she explain? She wasn't worried about the results of the shoot. She was worried that she and Jay wouldn't get through the shoot at all.

She entered the photo studio the following morning, forcing a smile and trying hard to adopt a carefree attitude. The twins were already there—two nineteen-year-old blondes from Atlanta, identical down to their eyelashes. Brenda and Bridget were stunning to look at, too, but neither of them had done any serious modeling.

Halley knew just how she wanted to market them. She knew the exact look she wanted to achieve. Communicating that look to the hair stylist and makeup artist was a breeze. Expressing her wants to Jay was going to be a whole lot harder.

By the time Jay arrived, the twins had been primped into perfect shape. They were clothed in identical body suits, which accentuated their well-proportioned figures.

Jay was anxious to get them in front of the camera, but Halley had other ideas. "We have to sit down together for a few minutes first," she told him firmly. "I have a very clear idea of what I want."

"Okay," he said, agreeably enough. They sat at a small table and chairs in the corner of the studio, and Halley launched into a twenty-minute explanation, complete with pages torn from magazines and complemented by her own sketches.

When she was finished, she took a deep breath. Jay leafed through the photos and sketches, his face etched into a deep scowl. "Is something wrong?" she asked, expecting an argument.

"No, I'll be happy to shoot it this way if you want."

"But?" she said for him.

He hesitated. "This is so . . . regimented, almost stiff."

"I know. I want it that way. I want to emphasize their symmetry."

"But the girls have such pretty smiles," he objected.

She gave him a challenging look.

"All right, never mind. Let's get started."

Halley caught herself holding her breath several times during the next two hours. Jay showed more skill than she'd given him credit for. The twins, nervous and fidgety at first, soon relaxed as he talked them through every moment. When he showed her the first proof, she was quite satisfied with the results and she relaxed.

She was forced to leave the studio for a few minutes to take a phone call. By the time she returned, the models were taking a break and Jay was examining a handful of proofs. She went directly to him and attempted to peer over his shoulder.

He turned and held the proofs to his chest, so she couldn't see. "I digressed a bit from your drawings," he warned her.

I will not lose my temper, she told herself, gritting her teeth. "Let me see," she said in a voice as even and mellow as she could muster.

She stared at the proofs, studied them with a supercritical eye. The first two were much as she'd envisioned. But by the third, the girls' rigid, symmetrical pose began to give way to a sinuous languor, a latent sexuality she hadn't dreamed possible with two such fresh-faced kids.

Something inside her wanted to find fault with what Jay had done. This was *her* studio, dammit, and her models. She was the one with the ideas. She was supposed to know best.

She couldn't find a blessed thing to complain about. Jay's photo was far superior to anything she'd envisioned.

She handed the proofs back to him. "They're very good, Jay," she said, enunciating every word so he couldn't possibly mistake them. "Forget my idea. Do this any way you like."

"No, Halley, I'm more than willing to go back to your original idea. I just wanted you to see—"

"Do it your way." She turned and stalked toward the exit.

He wasn't going to let her get away that easy. He trotted ahead of her, then stood in the exit, blocking her path. "You can't go away mad," he said firmly. Then, with less certainty, "Are you mad?"

She leaned her back against the wall and folded her arms, seeming to consider this question seriously. "I spend four hours coming up with an idea for this shoot, and you overrule me in five minutes. If that's not bad enough, your five-minute idea is ten times better than my four-hour one. Of course I'm angry."

"Sometimes it's just easier to see things when you're behind the camera," he mumbled.

In that moment, Halley realized he hadn't meant to take control away from her. He'd just done what came naturally. "I want you to do the shoot any way you see fit," she said again. "Really," she added at his dubious look. "I'm a little put out, but I'm not too dense to realize you know, better than me, what you're doing. I'll get over it."

He still looked a little doubtful.

"I'll get over it," she repeated. "I'm thinking of poisoning your meat loaf, but by tonight I'm sure I'll decide against it."

He smiled, and so did she, finally. He leaned down to kiss her forehead and she let him, despite the "hands-off" policy they'd agreed to follow while they worked together.

Halley stayed out of the studio the rest of the day, even after the Hankamer girls had been ushered into her office to sign their contracts. By five o'clock, Jay still hadn't called to tell her the final prints were ready for her inspection. She resisted the urge to check on him. She was learning to trust him, and that realization filled her with optimism.

She decided instead to go home and fix meat loaf—just to keep him on his toes.

It was dark by the time she made it home. As she mounted the short flight of stairs to the front door of the townhouse, she notice that the porch light was burned out. She was irritated at first, then a little spooked when she thought she saw one of the shadows move. She gripped her house keys more firmly in her hand as she moved resolutely toward the door, telling herself she was being silly.

"Halley?"

She jumped and dropped her keys at the sound of the soft voice, but the fear was quickly replaced by rage as she realized who was standing not two feet away from her.

"Harold Dempsey, where the hell have you been?"

Ten

"Hello," he greeted her, as if they'd just met casually on an elevator. "It took me awhile to find you. I didn't realize you'd still be living here . . . It's awfully cold. Can we go inside?"

"I don't believe this," Halley muttered as she retrieved the keys that had fallen at her feet, and unlocked the door. She didn't give Harold the chance to merely follow her inside. She grabbed him by the collar of his overcoat and dragged him behind her. She didn't stop until she'd escorted him into the living room and pushed him into a chair.

It didn't occur to her to be afraid of Harold. He might be a wanted felon, a fugitive from the FBI, but he was not dangerous in the slightest. In fact, Halley suspected that she herself had more of a capacity for violence than Harold, and at the moment she was hard put to suppress it.

She leaned over him, clutching his bow tie and almost

pulling him off the chair. "You worthless worm, why did you do it? Why did you steal from me?"

He tried to form words, but no sound came out. She released him, turning away in disgust.

"I never meant to hurt you, Halley," he said after a moment.

She turned on him again, swift as a cobra. "Hurt me? You almost destroyed me! You nearly bankrupted my business. If you didn't want to hurt me, you should have tried bamboo shoots under my fingernails." She moved toward the telephone. "I'm calling the police."

"I didn't . . ." She couldn't hear the rest, he'd spoken so softly.

"What?" Her hand froze, poised over the phone.

He squirmed a little. Halley could make out a faint sheen of perspiration on his bald head, despite the coolness of the room, and his glasses slid down his slick nose.

He pushed them up again. "I said I didn't take the money. Oh, I took some—little bits here and there, where you'd never miss it. But I would never have wiped you out like . . . like *she* did."

"*She?* She who?" Halley asked, though she was almost afraid to know the answer.

"My girlfriend," he answered matter-of-factly. "Ex-girlfriend, I should say."

Halley walked slowly to the sofa and sank into it, folding her arms tightly to keep from trembling. "Suppose you start at the beginning," she suggested.

"That's what I came here to do. Then you can call the police. I want to turn myself in."

He looked so miserable that Halley actually softened toward him. "I'm listening," she said.

"Well, a few months ago I started going out with a woman that I was pretty crazy about." He colored with embarrassment, but he went on. "She was beautiful, and glamorous—the kind of woman who wouldn't normally go for an ordinary guy like me. I guess I was so flattered I wasn't thinking straight, because when she came to me in trouble, asking for help, I gave it to her—anything within my power."

"What kind of trouble?" Halley asked.

"Money trouble. *Big* money trouble. She had borrowed from the wrong sort of people and she couldn't pay them back."

"Drugs?" Halley asked.

Harold shrugged. "I assume so. I didn't press her for details. They threatened to hurt her, Halley, and I just couldn't stand it. I gave her almost everything I had, and then some of what you had, and once I started I couldn't stop. No matter how much money I gave her, it was never enough."

He shook his head sadly. "My worst mistake was in telling her how I did it—how I embezzled. I suppose I wanted to impress her with how clever I was." He stopped, gazed around the room as if trying to collect his thoughts. His hands fidgeted in his lap.

"And then what happened?" Halley prompted, though she was pretty sure she knew the answer.

"She used the information I'd given her to pull her own scam. She forged my signature, did some fancy funds transferrals from account to account until she had all your money in cash. It's not something she did spur-of-the-moment. She had the whole thing planned. She was just using me. I was nothing but a . . . a pigeon."

He looked so miserable that Halley had a hard time maintaining her anger. "Why didn't you come to me right away?" she asked.

"I was so panicked when I found out what she'd done, I didn't know what to do. She said if I breathed a word to anyone, she'd be on a plane to South America with the money so fast my head would spin, and I believed her. She let me hide at her apartment. I was hoping that I could convince her to turn herself in, or at least return the money, but . . ." His voice trailed off.

"I take it she had no intention of mending her ways," Halley supplied.

Harold shook his head, a hopeless expression on his face. "When I read Cecily's column, I realized what a terrible mess you were in, and I had to do something. That's when I managed to steal some of the money back. She kept most of it in cash, you see, so that she wouldn't leave a paper trail. I cracked her safe when she wasn't home." He said this almost proudly.

"And you sent the money to me," Halley said, putting two and two together. "So *that's* where it came from."

He nodded eagerly. "I thought I'd find a lot more, but she'd either spent it or stashed it somewhere else." He paused, as if waiting for some sign of approval from Halley.

Her own head was spinning from this latest revelation. She battled with two emotions—elation that the anonymous cash was actually hers, and guilt over the way she'd accused Jay of sending it. Guilt won out. She'd actually branded Jay a liar! How could she be so lacking in perception? Jay would never lie to her, not about something as important as that.

"Anyway," Harold continued, interrupting her self-flagellation, "I finally decided to turn myself in the day she came home with that coat—your coat."

"So it was Maureen," Halley said, barely breathing the words. She had begun to suspect as much.

"I realized then that she wasn't merely greedy. She was out for revenge. She wanted to ruin you completely, and I couldn't let that happen."

"All because I refused to represent her?" Halley asked, incredulous.

"That was a big part of it. But she's out of control, and she really despises you, Halley. You had everything she ever wanted—youth, beauty, a successful business of your own, respect in the industry, a stable home life—she didn't know about your divorce. I didn't tell anyone, Halley. At least I kept that promise."

The secrecy about her divorce seemed silly now, Halley thought, shaking her head. Her priorities had changed, she supposed.

"That's about it," said Harold. "You can call the police now."

She nodded and wasted no time contacting Mr. Abrams from the FBI, the man who was in charge of her case. She explained briefly what Harold had told her about Maureen. Abrams assured Halley that someone would be there quickly to arrest Harold, and that Maureen's involvement would be investigated.

While they waited for the police to arrive, Halley offered Harold a diet cola and some homemade cookies Jay's mother had sent. The scene's irony brought her to the brink of laughter, but eating and drinking with Harold was better than simply staring at him.

Two officers arrived within fifteen minutes. They cuffed a docile Harold and took him away with little fanfare, and he looked so pitiful that Halley felt her throat constrict. He kept his eyes downcast, never once looking at her.

It was only when she was once again alone that she wondered what the repercussions of Harold's confession would be. Would she get the rest of her money back? Or would Maureen make good her threat and hustle herself off to Rio?

Halley was weary with worrying about it. Screaming her frustrations into Harold's face had rid her of most of her anger and resentment. At this point she didn't much care what happened, so long as the matter got settled one way or another.

A noise at the front door reminded her of a much more pressing concern. Jay was home, and she had some fence mending to do.

Outside on the porch, Jay fumbled with his key ring, frantic over what he'd just seen. He'd been walking home from the subway station, pleased with himself over the Hankamer twins' photos, when he'd noticed the flashing lights of a police car in front of the townhouse.

Still more than a block away, he'd broken into a sprint. Two officers were escorting a handcuffed man down the front steps and into the waiting car. He'd called out to them, but they'd sped off before he could stop them.

At last he got the proper key inserted into the lock and shoved the door open. "Halley?" he called out as he tumbled inside, his eyes seeking her out. When he spotted her in the living room, just rising from her chair to greet him, relief washed over him, a relief so profound that his knees almost buckled.

"Jay?" she said uncertainly. "Something wrong?"

He went to her quickly, pulling her into his arms before she could protest, hugging her too hard, he knew, but unable to stop himself. "Are you all right?" he demanded.

"Of course. What in the world's gotten into you?" Just the same, she hugged him back.

"What were the police doing here?" he asked. "Who was that man they took away?" He forced himself to release her, though he kept hold of one of her hands.

"That was Harold," she answered. "Don't worry, he came here only to apologize and to turn himself in."

"Harold, here?"

She smiled at his amazement. "It's a long story. I'll take you out to dinner and tell you all about it. How does Ling's sound?"

Food was the last thing on his mind. He was ashamed to admit, even to himself, how really frightened he'd been a few moments earlier. It was bad enough coming home every day, wondering if Halley had found another place to live and praying she hadn't, praying she'd still be here. The thought that he could lose her to something else—accident, illness, foul play—hadn't occurred to him until tonight. He gave an involuntary shiver.

"Jay?"

"Uh, sure, Ling's sounds fine."

"What's that you're holding?"

"What? Oh. The prints from today's shoot. Have a look." He handed her the envelope, at last feeling his wits returning along with some measure of calm.

"Oh, they're wonderful!" she exclaimed as she examined the prints, and she sounded genuinely delighted. "You used both of our ideas. I like it."

"I figured a compromise might not be so bad. Then when I compared the proofs side by side, I realized they made a dramatic contrast—better than either one of our ideas on their own."

"You know, you're right," Halley said. "I'll have to come up with a little different marketing angle...got any ideas?"

He could hardly believe his ears. She was actually asking for his advice. "I'll give it some thought," he said, trying to mask his delight with nonchalance. "But not on an empty stomach." He found he had an appetite after all.

Halley nodded in agreement as she laid the prints on the coffee table.

When she retrieved her wrap from the coat tree, he reflexively helped her on with it. Only then did he notice she was wearing her old cloth coat, and not her fur. "Where's the fox?" he asked, curious since he'd seldom seen her without it lately.

When she turned, he knew he'd hit a nerve. "I sold it to Maureen Argent."

"Oh, Halley." What else could he say? He knew how fond she'd been of the custom-made coat. He was tempted to chide her for not coming to him first, if she needed money that badly. After all, she'd promised to send out a distress signal if she got into a bind. He could have scraped something together. But she didn't need to hear a lecture. "It'll look terrible on Maureen," he finally said. "The color's all wrong for her."

Halley rewarded him with a laugh. "I'm surprised at you, Jay. I didn't know you could be so catty. And you know what I just realized? Maureen paid me for the coat with my own money. Now that's funny, even if it does make me feel like a fool." She laughed again.

Jay shook his head. "I don't understand."

"You will. Come on, let's get to Ling's before it gets too crowded."

At a secluded corner booth in their favorite Chinese restaurant, she told him the strange tale of how Maureen had used Harold to exact her revenge. Jay was so astonished that he left most of his food untouched—an almost unheard-of phenomenon.

"So does that mean you get your money back?" he asked.

She shrugged. "The FBI man said maybe, maybe not. A lot depends on whether they really have a case against Maureen and whether she cooperates. And she might have already spent it all. Well, not all," she corrected herself. "Jay, there's something I have to tell you."

"It's not anything shocking, is it?" he asked. "Because I've had about enough drama for one evening."

"No, nothing shocking," she assured him. "But it is something serious. I found out today that Harold sent that anonymous cash to me."

Jay leaned back against the banquette and folded his arms, well aware of what she was leading up to. And much as he hated to antagonize her, he deserved vindication in a big way and he was going to enjoy every minute of it. Though she'd long ago given up her anger over that envelope full of money and had even teased him about it, her lack of faith had hurt. "So?" he said, raising one eyebrow.

"So, obviously you didn't send the money, and I owe you a big fat apology."

He watched her fidget for a moment. "Yes, you do," he said, frowning ominously.

"I'm sorry. I should have known you wouldn't interfere so blatantly when you'd promised not to."

"And?"

"And I was wrong to believe you'd ever lie to me. Please forgive me."

He stabbed a water chestnut with his chopstick, then studied it carefully before popping it into his mouth. He chewed it slowly and swallowed before saying anything. "On one condition."

"Anything," she responded without hesitation. The fact that she trusted him not to ask the impossible touched him as nothing else could have.

"Tell me what you and your mother were talking about the other morning. Something to do with your father."

A wary look crossed her eyes before she answered. "I'll tell you," she said, "but why do you want to know?"

He shrugged. "Just a hunch."

She made herself more comfortable, tossing her napkin on the table and leaning back against the padded bench. "Did you know that my mother used to be a dancer?"

He nodded. "Cora mentioned it once."

"She wasn't just your average ballerina. She was one of the most promising members of the New York Metropolitan Ballet, fast on her way up. Then she met my father, fell in love, got married, and got pregnant—not necessarily in that order, mind you."

Jay took a moment to sort that out. "You mean you were a seven-month baby?" he asked, amused to think of the dignified, slightly plump Cora as an impetuous, passionate young woman.

"Well, yeah. That series of events pretty much axed her career. Physically she might have been able to return to dancing after I was born, but Dad lived and worked in rural Pennsylvania, and Mom never questioned that her place was at his side."

"That's pretty much the way it was back then, Halley," Jay commented.

"I know. But I think she regretted it sometimes. I caught her once in the attic, looking at her old scrapbook, tears streaming down her cheeks. She kept telling me it was just dust in her eyes."

"And some day, when you're older, you'll look at your modeling portfolio and cry, too. That's nostalgia, not necessarily regret."

"I haven't finished."

"Sorry. Go on."

"When I was in high school, Mom didn't have a lot to keep her busy, and she got this great idea to start a dance school. Dad thought it was a wonderful concept, and he backed her a hundred percent. He found a little storefront studio for her to rent, he helped her with her business plan and her advertising. He arranged a loan for her, to get her started." Halley paused to take a sip of tea.

Jay shifted uncomfortably. He knew what was coming.

"Everything went fine for a while," Halley continued. "I'd never seen my mother so excited about anything. It was like she'd recaptured a tiny piece of the dream she'd given up all those years ago and was eager to share it with her students. But when she didn't see a profit right away, my father started getting antsy.

"So Mom put in more hours at the studio, started a couple more classes. That meant she spent less time at home, so sometimes dinner was late and sometimes Dad couldn't find a pair of socks that matched because the laundry wasn't folded.

"And, well, he decided the dance school wasn't such a good idea after all, and he pulled the plug. Closed her down within a month."

Jay had watched as Halley grew more and more uncomfortable telling the story, until, when she was finished, she sat rigidly with her fists clenched and her face slightly flushed.

"What did your mother do?" he asked gently.

"Nothing! She insisted that she owed him her loyalty, for taking care of her and me all those years. And she just kept right on cooking his meals and cleaning up the house like nothing was wrong."

"And what did you do?"

"There wasn't much I *could* do, except get mad enough for the both of us." She took a deep breath and another sip of the cooling tea. "It still makes me mad."

"I can see that."

"It's silly," she said with a self-conscious laugh. "It happened fifteen years ago, and Mom has all but forgotten it. I should too, I guess, but I can't. It just sticks with me, for some reason."

Jay sighed. "Halley, why didn't you tell me this four, maybe five years ago?"

Her forehead creased in confusion. "I don't know. Is it that important?"

"It's obviously important to you. And it would have helped me to understand a few things about you."

She contemplated that, appearing unconvinced.

They were silent as the waitress cleared their table and brought them fortune cookies. Jay immediately picked one up and cracked it open, hoping to lighten the mood. He found the hidden fortune and scanned it, then groaned inwardly.

"What's it say?" Halley asked.

He cleared his throat. "Make peace with your adversary."

"Does that mean you forgive me?" she asked, completely serious.

He reached across the table and touched her face, lightly. "I don't know. Are you my adversary?"

"Sometimes," she acknowledged with a reflective smile.

"Then I guess you're forgiven. Now read your fortune."

She shook her head. "I don't like fortune cookies."

"You don't have to eat the damn thing, just look at the fortune."

"No. Let's quit while we're ahead." She picked up the bill and scooted out of the booth, and he had no choice but to follow.

After she paid for their meal at the cash register, Halley handed some folded bills to Jay. "I forgot to leave a tip," she said. "Would you run back to the table while I go to the ladies' room?"

"Sure." When he'd returned to the table and set the bills under the soy sauce, he couldn't resist cracking open Halley's cookie. He read the message and was infinitely relieved she hadn't seen it.

"Soon you will enjoy a new home." That was one fortune he hoped wouldn't come true.

Several days later, sitting in the agency's foyer with Kathryn, Halley read aloud a newspaper account of Maureen's arrest. The story gave her little satisfaction. Though she was elated that a good portion of the embezzled funds had been recovered and would soon be at her disposal once again, she was saddened that Maureen had allowed petty revenge to ruin her life.

"I knew there was some reason I didn't like her," Kathryn commented.

Halley shook her head. "I should have listened to you, I guess."

"Well, at least you never agreed to represent her."

Halley remained silent, unwilling to admit that only last week she had almost begged Maureen to join the agency. It had been a stupid thing to do, she knew now. She'd never again ignore her instincts on such a matter.

Changing the subject, Kathryn asked, "When will Betty finish the financial statement?"

Halley brightened. "Should be any time." Betty Loggins had come highly recommended as a financial trouble-shooter, and Halley could think of no one's accounts in more trouble than hers had been. She'd been taking care of the books herself since Harold's departure, and her skills in that area were minimal.

A couple of days ago Betty had accompanied Halley to the bank, to straighten out her debts and reassure the ever-vigilant Ms. Winsome that the agency's finances were on the upswing. Now Betty was working on a comprehensive financial statement that hopefully would show Halley just what shape the agency was in.

If Betty's work proved satisfactory, Halley planned to hire her as a permanent financial consultant to take over some of Harold's old duties.

"And the new photographer, that friend of Peg Zimmerman's? When is he starting?" Kathryn asked.

"Not till next week, I'm afraid," Halley replied. "And we can't depend on Jay or Peg anymore. The insurance company settled on their claim, and today they're out shopping for new cameras and whatnot."

"They got us pretty well caught up, didn't they?" Kathryn asked.

Halley nodded. Her brief business association with Jay hadn't turned into the disaster she'd feared. Uncomfortable though it was, the temporary arrangement had helped them both through a dilemma. Now that it was over, and Jay had eagerly relinquished control of the studio, she felt nothing but relief.

When Betty Loggins arrived, Halley couldn't begin to guess the results of her audit by the impassive look on the woman's sturdy, no-nonsense face. So Halley led the way into the conference room, braced for the worst.

"Well, Ms. Jernigan," Betty began, "you should be quite proud of yourself."

"I should?" Halley asked idiotically.

"It's a miracle you held this business together, under the circumstances. Most CEOs in your position would have chucked out the whole mess and started over. Few would have risked their personal finances to bail out what appeared from all sides to be a losing proposition. I honestly don't know how you managed it. To have that much faith in a company, and in your own abilities, is rare."

"And maybe not so smart?" Halley added.

Betty gave her an enigmatic look. "By declaring bankruptcy, you would have done irreversible damage to your future in this industry. As it is you've cracked your public image a bit, but it's nothing that can't be fixed. In a few months your track record should speak for itself."

Halley was impressed with the extent of this woman's knowledge of the subtle aspects of the fashion industry. She was much more than a number cruncher. "Then you're saying I have a future?" she ventured. She'd been half afraid that Betty would advise her to give up.

"Oh my, yes," the accountant said with a rare smile. "Let me show you what I've come up with..."

They pored over the numbers for more than an hour. By the time they were done, Halley was stunned. Even with the loss of business brought on by the negative publicity, and even though some of the embezzled funds would never be recovered, the agency's finances had made an amazing turnaround.

"I just have one question," Betty said. "This five thousand dollars here, which shows up on the fifth of February. I can't for the life of me figure out where it came from."

"I, um, sold a personal investment," Halley mumbled, unwilling to admit that she'd accepted her own money for her fur coat.

"Ah, then we need to return that to your personal account."

"Can the agency afford to do that?" Halley asked.

"I expect so—at least by the first of the month," Betty answered matter-of-factly.

After the accountant left, Halley stared at the statement, letting the bottom line sink into her brain. All the scrambling and scraping she and Kathryn had done, all the collecting, all the cost-cutting measures, had paid off in a big way. The Cyndi-O account, which she'd finally nabbed once and for all, hadn't hurt things, either.

Fact was, she was downright flush.

Eleven

With Halley's newly recovered wealth came an unpleasant realization: There was no need for her to remain in Jay's townhouse, now that she could afford her own place.

The posh Upper East Side, where she'd found an apartment before, held no appeal for her now. Such blatant opulence flew in the face of her newly developed reverence for economy. She'd never again feel as blithely secure about money as she had when she'd agreed to rent that luxurious flat.

If she had to move, a cozy little place in Murray Hill, or even Gramercy Park, was more her speed, she decided, though she didn't want to move at all.

Halley was convinced she and Jay were ready to try again. So far, they'd merely been making the best of an awkward situation. The next logical step, in her mind at least, was for them to commit to a real reconciliation.

The problem was, she didn't know what was in Jay's mind. They hadn't managed a lot of time together the last few days. Halley's new accounts and new models were demanding much of her attention, and Jay was making up for all the time he'd lost as a result of the burglary.

That was a pattern she didn't like. Hectic work schedules hadn't done their marriage any good. It was time for her, at least, to put some of her agency's demands into the capable hands of her staff. She now knew she could let go of some of her responsibilities.

Still, she forced herself to read the apartment want ads during a solitary lunch in her office. Until she learned otherwise, she would have to assume that sooner or later, she'd be moving to a place of her own.

She hadn't yet told Jay just how healthy her budget had become. She'd been putting it off, she admitted with a twinge of guilt. When he found out about her new financial independence, they would have to reach a decision about living arrangements.

How *would* he react, Halley wondered, when he found out? Though she wasn't privy to Jay's bank book, she had a fair idea of where he stood. She was pretty sure she'd soon be making more money than he was. How would he handle it?

All of the progress they'd made had stemmed directly from her unfortunate predicament and his unique capacity to come to her rescue. Now that she was out of the woods, she was about to face the one change of circumstance that had the power to blow their relationship out of the water. With the status quo restored, would they revert to their old, destructive patterns?

Things were different this time around, she reminded herself. She had made Jay an integral part of her success. He was no longer an outsider where her agency was concerned. And she'd learned to accept that fact—not as gracefully as was ideal, perhaps, but she was working on that.

She sighed. Asking herself all these questions was pointless. She'd never know the answers until she talked to Jay.

Halley didn't know whether to feel lucky or cursed when she located a suitable apartment almost immediately. It was a beautiful, roomy two-bedroom in a charming Murray Hill neighborhood, with a small balcony overlooking a courtyard. Kathryn had found it for her—bless her well-meaning heart.

The place was perfect, yet Halley could not muster one iota of enthusiasm for it. She told the eager rental agent that she would look over the lease that night and let her know in the morning.

The time had come to confront Jay and face whatever truths awaited her.

After dumping the rest of the day's work on a loudly protesting Peg, Jay left the studio shortly after lunch. "I'll make it up to you," he promised breezily as he scooted out the door. Right now he had business to attend to that wouldn't wait.

Last night he'd reached a decision. He hadn't wanted to pressure Halley about their future. Her work was giving her a lot to contend with right now, and it hadn't seemed appropriate to broach the subject of her living quarters when she had so much else on her mind.

But last night he'd seen that telltale newspaper page sticking out of her coat pocket. Want ads. She was looking for an apartment again.

He could talk to her about it, but he'd never been all that good with words. He smiled as he remembered the other morning, when he'd made the craziest, most passionate, *quickest* love to her he could remember. He was always more successful at showing Halley how he felt, rather than telling her. That thought gave him confidence. He was doing the right thing.

By the time Halley arrived home that evening, Jay had everything ready. A bottle of wine was chilling in the fridge, and a pizza—her favorite kind—was warming in the oven.

A large box sat on the coffee table, waiting for her. And the rest of the house was…well, he'd wait and see how long it took her to figure it out.

She seemed surprised to find him at home, though it was already close to seven.

"I guess I've been putting in some long hours," he said, "but we're almost caught up. Things should get back to normal soon."

"Same here," she said.

When he kissed her forehead, he noted the lines of tension, and the tightness in her pursed lips. He kissed her there, too, relentlessly, until he felt her relax a little.

She was working too hard again, but he resisted the urge to say something. Now that he'd had a firsthand look at her business, he could see how essential she was to it. She couldn't shortchange the Mystique Agency if it needed her time, and he had no right to expect her to.

He *could* insist that she eat right and get her rest, he mused, thinking guilty thoughts about the pizza.

"Want some wine?" he asked casually.

"Love some," she replied automatically. Something was up, she thought as she took off her coat. Jay was as edgy as a kid waiting to see the dentist. Whatever it was, it would surface soon. He was terrible at keeping secrets. Anyway, she was in no hurry to reveal her own news—no hurry at all.

They settled onto the couch in the living room to enjoy the wine, and Jay slipped his arm around her. She leaned her head on his shoulder, grateful for his warmth and strength. She hoped maybe she would absorb some of it. She didn't relish the task ahead of her.

"Tough day?" he asked.

"Oh, no tougher than—what's that?" she asked, pointing to the box on the coffee table.

"That's something for you," he said nonchalantly.

Aha, she thought, moving to examine it. This had something to do with why Jay was so nervous. Unable to even imagine what she'd find, she knelt beside the coffee table and gingerly lifted the lid off the box.

Instantly she recognized the bluish-gray fur peaking out from the tissue paper. Just to be sure, she lifted the garment from its nest and shook it out. It was her coat, all right. There wasn't another one like it in the world.

She looked back at Jay, finding her words difficult. When she finally could speak, she said, "You didn't pay money for this, did you?" She was thinking of the fact that she'd already paid for the damn thing twice.

Obviously that wasn't the reaction he'd been looking for, because she could clearly see the disappointment in his eyes. "Uh, fortunately, no. I went to visit Maureen today. She's out on bond, you know. I asked her to return the coat."

"And she agreed?" Halley could hardly believe that.

"I convinced her that she might get a lighter sentence if she showed some remorse for her crime. That's all it took."

Halley returned her attention to the coat. Though she was touched by the effort Jay had made to retrieve it for her, she was amazed to discover she really didn't want it back. What she'd once seen as the very essence of success now seemed only a shallow symbol. She measured success differently these days.

To please him, she slipped her arms into the sleeves of the fox coat and wrapped it around her. "Thank you, Jay," she said, blinking back tears. "You were brave. You faced a real live dragon for me."

He shrugged. "I'd do anything for you. Or nothing at all, if that's what you want."

He was trying so hard, and she loved him so much for it. But she had a small matter to take care of before she turned into a blubbering, sentimental idiot. "I have something to show you," she said decisively, moving briskly toward her briefcase, which she'd left in the entry hall. When she'd retrieved the necessary papers and returned to the living room, she found Jay pacing nervously.

She was filled with longing for him, and with a terrible fear that she'd lose him. Briefly, she considered putting off her revelation awhile longer, but the suspense of not knowing was more than she could bear.

Staving off her desire, she pressed the papers into his hand. After a momentary expression of surprise, he studied the first one—a personal check made out to him for fifteen hundred dollars. He looked at her quizzically.

"It's half of what I owe you for that Visa bill you paid off. The rest will come next month." She waited, expecting him to argue.

"Are you sure you can afford it comfortably?" he asked, still contemplating the amount of the check.

"Yes. The other paper is my latest financial statement. I'd like you to look it over while I, um, change my clothes." *Chicken,* she berated herself as she made a quick exit and headed for the guest room. She was too scared to watch him read it.

"Halley?" he called out to her.

She froze. "Yes?"

"You won't find your clothes in there."

What was he talking about? She entered the room that had been hers for the past month and was stunned by the emptiness. The dresser was bare of her familiar perfume bottles and other clutter. There were no shoes kicked into the corner, no nightgown draped over the arm of the sofa bed.

He didn't, she thought. He wouldn't really do this without asking, would he?

She marched out the door, across the hall and into the master bedroom. There were all her things, cozied up next to Jay's, looking as if she'd never packed them up in the first place.

She opened the closet, not at all surprised to find her sweaters and wool suits occupying their old spaces. Her lingerie was tucked neatly into the top drawer of the dresser.

Her slippers peeked out from under the bed. And lying on *top* of the neatly made bed, draped across her pillow, was her sexiest black nightie. The whole effect was a little eerie, as if the divorce had been nothing more than a bad dream.

How dare he!

She shot out of the bedroom like a torpedo and returned to where Jay stood in the middle of the living room, intently studying the enlightening piece of paper. Her boxes, which had remained stacked against the walls all this time, had vanished. She folded her arms, waiting for him to look up. Her foot tapped a staccato rhythm against the wood floor.

The nerve, she seethed. Where did he find the gall to unpack her boxes without her consent? The decision to remain here should have been hers. How could he be so arrogant as to make that choice for her? Hadn't he learned anything?

She took off the fur and laid it over the back of the sofa, then pushed up her sweater sleeves, prepared to do battle.

Jay's unrestrained whoop startled her so thoroughly that it took the steam out of her engine. He looked up, saw her, and grinned like a Cheshire cat. "You better come here. I can't wait much longer."

"Wait for what?" she asked, approaching cautiously.

He took two giant steps, closing the distance between them. "For this." He hugged her to him, hard, then lifted her and twirled her around effortlessly. "Congratulations, babe. You did it."

Whatever momentary anger she'd felt evaporated like a mist. "No, *we* did it," she corrected him, ruffling his blond hair as joy and relief shimmered through her. If Jay felt threatened by her finances or envious of her success, he sure knew how to hide it. He was beaming like a lighthouse.

"I may have helped, a little," he admitted. "But you're the one—Halley, I just can't believe how you've turned things around!"

"It's pretty amazing, all right," she agreed.

"I guess you can afford that Park Avenue penthouse now," he said, sounding not quite as elated as he had a moment before.

She stiffened. *He changed his mind,* her panicky mind echoed. *He wants me to leave after all....*

"I knew you were looking," he said softly. "I don't intend to make it easy for you to move out, you know. I unpacked every one of those damn boxes, and so help me I crushed the empties and took them to the curb, so you wouldn't repack them."

"Thank heavens! I don't want to move out," she assured him, melting back into his embrace.

"You don't?"

"I love you, Jay, and I want us to try again. But I was afraid of what you'd say when you saw that statement. I'm still a little afraid. Now that I won't be depending on you for monetary support..." Her voice trailed off.

"It doesn't matter. It's you I love, not your work, not your money or lack thereof. And I promise, from now on I'll stay out of your business. I'll accept whatever career you choose, and I'll respect whatever degree of independence you want."

Smiling, Halley resisted the urge to point out the contradiction between his words and his recent actions. What did a few piddley unpacked boxes matter, anyway?

"I know we'll have some tough times," he said, cautiously.

"Oh, I'm sure," she agreed. "We still have some adjustments to make."

"And we're still learning new things about each other, even after all these years."

"I know. I hope we never stop learning."

"But we've got more than enough love between us to get us through those rough spots, don't you think?"

She nodded against his shoulder.

"That's why I think we should get married again."

Startled, she pulled back to look at him. "Really?" she squeaked. She hadn't gotten that far in her thinking. She'd just assumed they'd live together and work from there. Maybe a second wedding hadn't occurred to her because she'd never really felt divorced in the first place.

"If we're going to commit to this thing, let's go all the way," Jay said. He tipped her chin up, caressed her cheek, her hair. "Marry me, Halley."

She felt caught in a whirlwind. In her dreams she'd never imagined that things would move this quickly, and she was unprepared. Her brain told her to proceed with caution.

Her heart, however, had other ideas. Jay had just offered her everything she could ever hope for. She would be crazy to turn it down.

"I know just the sort of ring I'd like to buy for you," he said when she didn't answer. "I'll have my client, that crazy jeweler, design one just for you. A blue topaz, to match your eyes."

"I like my old ring," she protested, thinking of the lovely pear-shaped diamond tucked away in her jewelry box.

"We need a new ring for a new start."

She shook her head. "It's not a new start. We're building on everything that went before. We've learned so much, and I don't want to forget any of it—even the hard times."

He smiled indulgently. "This is no time to argue. Whatever ring you want to wear is fine." The smile faded. "I haven't heard you say yes."

She saw all the love and pride in Jay's eyes as he waited patiently for her answer, and she knew she was succeeding in every way that mattered. "Yes," she breathed. And then she kissed him, long and hard.

* * * * *

SILHOUETTE'S "BIG WIN"
SWEEPSTAKES RULES & REGULATIONS
NO PURCHASE NECESSARY TO ENTER OR RECEIVE A PRIZE

1. To enter the Sweepstakes and join the Reader Service, scratch off the metallic strips on all your BIG WIN tickets #1-#6. This will reveal the potential values for each Sweepstakes entry number, the number of free book(s) you will receive and your free bonus gift as part of our Reader Service. If you do not wish to take advantage of our Reader Service but wish to enter the Sweepstakes only, scratch off the metallic strips on your BIG WIN tickets #1-#4. Return your entire sheet of tickets intact. Incomplete and/or inaccurate entries are ineligible for that section or sections of prizes. Torstar Corp. and its affiliates are not responsible for mutilated or unreadable entries or inadvertent printing errors. Mechanically reproduced entries are null and void.

2. Whether you take advantage of this offer or not, on or about April 30, 1992, at the offices of Marden-Kane Inc., Lake Success, NY, your Sweepstakes numbers will be compared against the list of winning numbers generated at random by the computer. However, prizes will only be awarded to individuals who have entered the Sweepstakes. In the event that all prizes are not claimed, a random drawing will be held from all qualified entries received from March 30, 1990 to March 31, 1992, to award all unclaimed prizes. All cash prizes (Grand to Sixth), will be mailed to the winners and are payable by check in U.S. funds. Seventh Prize will be shipped to winners via third-class mail. These prizes are in addition to any free, surprise or mystery gifts that might be offered. Versions of this Sweepstakes with different prizes of approximate equal value may appear at retail outlets or in other mailings by Torstar Corp. and its affiliates.

3. The following prizes are awarded in this sweepstakes: ★ Grand Prize (1) $1,000,000; First Prize (1) $25,000; Second Prize (1) $10,000; Third Prize (5) $5,000; Fourth Prize (10) $1,000; Fifth Prize (100) $250; Sixth Prize (2,500) $10; ★ ★ Seventh Prize (6,000) $12.95 ARV.

   ★ This presentation offers a Grand Prize of a $1,000,000 annuity. Winner will receive $33,333.33 a year for 30 years without interest totalling $1,000,000.

   ★ ★ Seventh Prize: A fully illustrated hardcover book published by Torstar Corp. Approximate Retail Value of the book is $12.95.

   Entrants may cancel the Reader Service at anytime without cost or obligation to buy (see details in center insert card).

4. This Sweepstakes is being conducted under the supervision of an independent judging organization. By entering this Sweepstakes, each entrant accepts and agrees to be bound by these rules and the decisions of the judges, which shall be final and binding. Odds of winning in the random drawing are dependent upon the total number of entries received. Taxes, if any, are the sole responsibility of the winners. Prizes are nontransferable. All entries must be received at the address printed on the reply card and must be postmarked no later than 12:00 MIDNIGHT on March 31, 1992. The drawing for all unclaimed Sweepstakes prizes will take place on May 30, 1992, at 12:00 NOON, at the offices of Marden-Kane, Inc., Lake Success, New York.

5. This offer is open to residents of the U.S., the United Kingdom, France and Canada, 18 years or older, except employees and their immediate family members of Torstar Corp., its affiliates, subsidiaries, and all the other agencies, entities and persons connected with the use, marketing or conduct of this Sweepstakes. All Federal, State, Provincial and local laws apply. Void wherever prohibited or restricted by law. Any litigation within the Province of Quebec respecting the conduct and awarding of a prize in this publicity contest must be submitted to the Régie des Loteries et Courses du Québec.

6. Winners will be notified by mail and may be required to execute an affidavit of eligibility and release, which must be returned within 14 days after notification or an alternate winner will be selected. Canadian winners will be required to correctly answer an arithmetical skill-testing question administered by mail, which must be returned within a limited time. Winners consent to the use of their names, photographs and/or likenesses for advertising and publicity in conjunction with this and similar promotions without additional compensation. For a list of our major prize winners, send a stamped, self-addressed ENVELOPE to: WINNERS LIST, c/o Marden-Kane Inc., P.O. Box 701, SAYREVILLE, NJ 08871 Requests for Winners Lists will be fulfilled after the May 30, 1992 drawing date.

If Sweepstakes entry form is missing, please print your name and address on a 3″ ×5″ piece of plain paper and send to:

In the U.S.
Silhouette's "BIG WIN" Sweepstakes
3010 Walden Ave.
P.O. Box 1867
Buffalo, NY 14269-1867

In Canada
Silhouette's "BIG WIN" Sweepstakes
P.O. Box 609
Fort Erie, Ontario
L2A 5X3

Offer limited to one per household.
© 1991 Harlequin Enterprises Limited   Printed in the U.S.A.

LTY-S391D

SILHOUETTE·INTIMATE·MOMENTS®

NORA ROBERTS
Night Shadow

People all over the city of Urbana were asking, Who was that masked man?

Assistant district attorney Deborah O'Roarke was the first to learn his secret identity . . . and her life would never be the same.

The stories of the lives and loves of the O'Roarke sisters began in January 1991 with NIGHT SHIFT, Silhouette Intimate Moments #365. And if you want to know more about Deborah and the man behind the mask, look for NIGHT SHADOW, Silhouette Intimate Moments #373.

Available now at your favorite retail outlet, or order your copy by sending your name, address, zip or postal code along with a check or money order for $2.95 (please do not send cash), plus 75¢ postage and handling, payable to Silhouette Reader Service to:

In the U.S.	In Canada
3010 Walden Ave.	P.O. Box 609
P.O. Box 1396	Fort Erie, Ontario
Buffalo, NY 14269-1396	L2A 5X3

Please specify book title(s) with your order.

Canadian residents add applicable federal and provincial taxes.

NITE-1A

Silhouette Books®